The Frankenstein Diaries

The Frankenstein Diaries

Translated from the original German and edited by
The Reverend Hubert Venables

A Charles Herridge Book

published by
Hutchinson

London Melbourne Sydney Auckland Johannesburg

Hutchinson & Co. (Publishers) Ltd

An imprint of the Hutchinson Publishing Group

3 Fitzroy Square, London W1P 6JD

Hutchinson Group (Australia) Pty Ltd
30-32 Cremorne Street, Richmond South, Victoria 3121
PO Box 151, Broadway, New South Wales 2007

Hutchinson Group (NZ) Ltd
32-34 View Road, PO Box 40-086, Glenfield, Auckland 10

Hutchinson Group (SA) Pty Ltd
PO Box 337, Bergvlei 2012, South Africa

First published 1980

© Copyright Charles Herridge Limited 1980
All rights reserved
Produced by Charles Herridge Ltd
Tower House, Abbotsham, Devon
Designed by Bruce Aiken
Typeset by Toptown Printers Ltd,
Barnstaple, Devon
Printed in Italy by
Officine Grafiche A. Mondadori, Verona
ISBN 0 09 142670 7

In friendship and in gratitude,
this modest work is
dedicated to my untiring
amanuensis, Stewart Cowley

Editor's Foreword

The tattered bundle of ancient, decaying papers arrived ten years ago from a colleague in Switzerland well acquainted with my enthusiasm for eighteenth-century German manuscripts. At that time, however, my pastoral duties precluded any lengthy personal divertissement and I consigned the parcel to a cupboard until I had more hours to hand.

Following my retirement, my desire to occupy the days with some useful and absorbing project brought the documents to mind once more, and retrieving the fragile sheets, I began to examine them closely. They were in poor condition and great disarray but the contents revealed by my first cursory study encouraged me to embark upon the prodigious task of collating and translating them.

Regrettably, a number of folios are entirely missing, while time and accident have made others indecipherable, either wholly or in part. Enough has survived, however, to represent the account of a truly extraordinary endeavour. In making this translation I have been forced to employ my reasoned judgement in filling in some of the more obvious omissions, though only in respect of matters of chronology or sequence. As I am not so qualified, I have made no attempt to reconstruct or presuppose any missing passages of a scientific nature, preferring to present the texts as they stand.

The work at last completed, I was free to deliberate upon the result. Though I was unwilling to believe that the history was anything other than a strange and sinister fiction, some quality in its presentation compelled me to seek elsewhere for some substantiation. My subsequent researches in the archives in Germany and Switzerland have obliged me to revise my opinion, in that I have established beyond all personal doubt the authenticity of the diaries as a true historical record of fact. in consequence I have suffered considerable anguish as to whether or not I should offer them for publication, for my own beliefs stand in utter opposition to those sentiments and intentions expressed by the author. Nevertheless I have decided that the issues involved are of greater import than I am qualified to suppress, and that it must fall unto each man to pass his own judgement, for whatever the verdict the moral will stand unchanged.

H. StJ.V.
York, 1980

Contents

The only known portrait of Viktor Frankenstein, probably made during his convalescence at Ingolstadt. It is possible that the artist was his close friend, Henri Clerval. This handsome, thoughtful visage betrays no hint of the madness that was later to assail him.

Prologue

The reader is bound to view with some scepticism the publication, over 150 years after the event, of a volume purporting to contain extracts from the diaries of a figure universally considered never to have lived. My own initial reaction was no different.

Yet there is some truth in the saying that there is no smoke without fire, or, more appropriately, that there is often if not usually a basis in real life for a legend. Encouraged by this thought, and with nothing but time to lose, I therefore began my investigations. With names, places and dates gleaned from examination of the papers, I was first able to establish, through parish records, the existence of an emigré family named Frankenstein in Geneva in the latter part of the eighteenth century.

The history of this family is in itself unexceptional, but because it produced in Viktor an evidently exceptional man, I offer it for what it is worth.

It appears that the family had until the fifteenth century owned substantial estates in Northern Bavaria (originally known as Franken). Being Lutherans they suffered persecution as a result of the Counter-Reformation that was sweeping through nearby Bohemia and fled to Geneva, already a sanctuary for the Calvinists and other religious groups, settling there to make their lives anew.

The tone of subsequent generations was one of solid respectability, the family becoming closely associated with the legal profession and providing Genevese society with a succession of lawyers, counsellors and magistrates. Wilhelm Frankenstein, father of Viktor, the author of these diaries, had also followed in the family tradition and was a respected, serious-minded magistrate who devoted his life to public service, marrying only quite late in his life. His wife, Caroline Beaufort, was the daughter of a long-standing merchant friend of the family. She bore Wilhelm three sons before her death from scarlet fever after only eighteen years of marriage: Viktor, Ernest (seven years later) and then William.

There is no doubt that Viktor was an infant prodigy and that his parents did much to encourage his development, as ample records exist to illustrate his remarkable abilities. The household accounts, for example, note the employment of a tutor when Viktor was about three years old, retained to 'instruct Viktor in writing, the principles of mathematics and to improve upon his reading'. Little more than a year later a letter from their holiday house by the lake from Wilhelm and Viktor to Caroline mentions Viktor's extensive collection of plant specimens and includes a number of drawings of his latest acquisitions.

A portrait of Caroline Beaufort, Viktor's mother, who died of scarlet fever in his eighteenth year, precipitating a nervous crisis.

The writings of the natural philosopher Paracelsus, depicted here in a painting by Rubens, played a vital part in setting the young Frankenstein on the road to scientific discovery.

A page from Viktor's childhood sketchbook showing one of his botanical studies.

The Frankensteins' attempts to educate their eldest son within the normal educational framework proved fruitless, as it was unable to provide for his exceptional talents, and, aware of his precocious leanings towards the sciences, they placed his instruction in the hands of private teachers who introduced him to the systematic techniques of eighteenth-century scientific research.

This was an important turning point for Viktor, and his natural facility for careful observation and systematic analysis allowed him to make astonishing progress in the fields of botany, chemistry, mathematics and related areas. In the hope of encouraging him to follow a medical career, his parents applied successfully for a scholarship to Ingolstadt University, but his entry was delayed by the period of his mother's fatal illness. Her death was a severe blow to Viktor, who became so distracted by the

A page from an early sketch-book showing the dissection of a rat performed by Viktor as a child.

tragedy that his family were concerned for his health. One letter from a Genevese specialist suggested 'the family must consider the possibility that Viktor might succumb physically to the melancholy which afflicts him. A mind so doubly active burns great quantities of the vital Principle and can itself be extinguished or made mad by a surfeit of spiritual ferment', a statement that was unintentionally prophetic.

The consuming inquisitiveness that had marked Viktor's childhood proved, however, to be more powerful than his acute depression, and after several weeks he expressed the desire to enrol at the university in order to study anatomy and physiology, never again making any mention of his mother. He was seventeen when he attended his first class, and his industry and enthusiasm soon brought him to the attention of the senior staff, notably that of a M. Waldman, a distinguished chemist and one of the faculty's foremost instructors. His recognition of Viktor's potential was the second important point in the young Frankenstein's development, for unlike previous mentors he encouraged him to pursue his own projects, intervening only to advise on procedure or to direct the youth to comparable work already recorded. As a result, Frankenstein was able to explore and experiment with a wider variety of subjects than was usually permitted, and to view them as inter-related fields instead of isolated disciplines. The results often led him into heated exchanges with less liberal members of the staff, and on more than one occasion accusations of blasphemy almost led to his expulsion from the University.

Nevertheless, his rapid progress and almost obsessive diligence were undeniable, and within two years he had begun to outstrip the resources of the college. He showed little interest in the university's social life and worked in an increasing isolation which even M. Waldman was eventually unable to penetrate. It was during this period that Viktor began to keep the diaries, recording both details of his work and his personal thoughts. His genius had always isolated him from his contemporaries, his youth from his intellectual peers, and the diaries became an increasingly important outlet for his innermost thoughts. Consequently, they represent not only a unique record of his scientific work but also the dramatic story of a solitary, dedicated mind fighting a terrifying battle against the forces of emotional chaos.

His studies led him down untrodden paths to places which in some cases are only now being visited. In earlier times his discoveries would probably have led to his execution for heresy. As it was, he could not entirely escape the moral climate of his age, and much of his agony was the result of the conflict between his consuming thirst for scientific enlightenment and his social conditioning. He had after all been denied a normal life from the very beginning and the pressures imposed by his own intellect had denied him the opportunity to acquire emotional experience and balance, with the result that the sophistication of his academic brain contrasted dangerously with a pronounced emotional naivety which was to play an ever more disturbing part in his life.

These diaries stand as a vivid record of a mind out of time.

This engraving of Professor Waldman was found in the archives of Ingolstadt University. A distinguished chemist and theoretician, he was quick to recognise the spark of genius in Viktor. It was through his influence that Viktor was allowed to pursue his own course of study.

A Mind Out of Time

'The entire world of scientific philosophy is founded on the fundamental understanding that Man is obliged to pursue Truth as if it were an independent beast inhabiting the forests of ignorance. I find it hard to accept this diminution of our intellectual stature, and would rather propose that the very creation of Truth is within our powers. There are moments when a power pulses in the darkness of my inner being which I firmly believe to be enough to create a reality where none existed before. We are at least the equal of Nature in that we already possess the power to alter or undo her laws. I believe that we can also choose to create further laws of our own which are unique and independent of any in Nature.'

Blasphemous and arrogant as this statement appears to be, it was, as one of Viktor's earliest diary entries, an

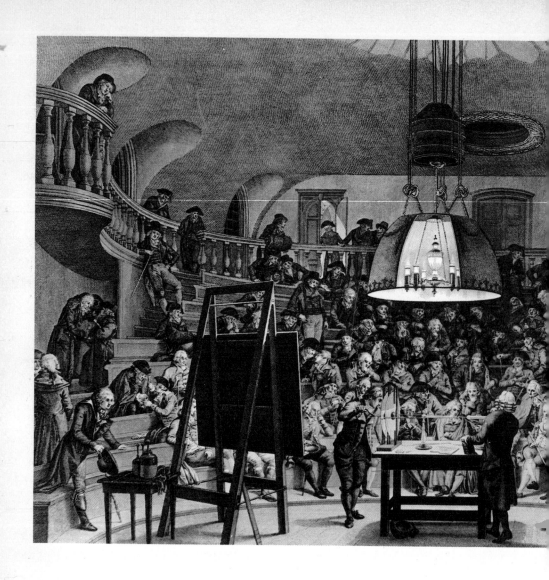

The Physical Sciences lecture theatre at Ingolstadt which was closely modelled on that of the University of Amsterdam. Under Professor Waldman's guidance, Ingolstadt became an important centre for the study of electricity, which provided Viktor with a sound basis for his researches into the nature of electro-magnetism.

important indication of his motivation and a conclusion drawn from a prodigious knowledge of the workings of Nature. By the time he had written this, he had travelled further along the path of knowledge than any of his contemporaries and had ventured into areas of study that had not even been conceived elsewhere. He played no active part in the affairs of the university but his pale, haunted face became as much a part of the campus landscape as the masonry itself as he laboured without respite in the laboratory provided.

'Whereas it is enough for other men to poke and prod at the hide of Nature, describing its limbs and counting the hairs on its pelt, I will not be content until I possess the power to enter its very soul, to become the conscience that directs its energies in the service of mankind. Death,

disease and natural despair will be banished from the world and Man will more closely reflect the image of his Maker.'

Turning thus away from the traditional methods of investigative study, Viktor devoted his considerable energies to the manipulation of the natural forces that had been proved to exist in Nature.

'I can no longer content myself with the science of my fellows, and like them peer into the twilight realm of natural phenomena to report the activities therein as studious scibes or clerks of some supernatural court. Though I do not profess myself completely versed in natural lore, I know enough to see that the path to enlightenment does not lie in that direction, but rather

Albrecht von Haller was probably the greatest figure in 18th century medical science, and for a time Viktor recognised in him a kindred spirit. Von Haller had also been an infant prodigy whose advanced ideas often set him apart from his scientific colleagues.

passes through landscapes where only the traveller who can command the forces of life may pass. And to command a horse does not require intimate knowledge of its anatomy, only the ability to impose the rider's will upon it. So must it be with science, and I am entirely resolved to govern the fundamental forces of life in order to bend them to the will of Man.'

He now began the series of experiments on the effects of various agencies on living plant and animal tissue that was to transform his life. He started by pursuing two parallel courses of study, the first being the detailed examination of the nature of cellular matter and its method of reproduction, and the second the effect of electricity on living matter. This latter interest was inspired by a casual remark made by M. Waldman who, during a discussion on the work of Galvani, Volta and the young Faraday, suggested that, 'The invisible power of electricity is of such subtlety that it could act upon the minutest essences of chemical matter to alter or govern its properties as well as manipulate its mass*'

* This last statement refers to Galvani's experiments in muscular stimulation as well as to the process of electro-magnetism.

On September 23rd Viktor wrote:

'There is much evidence that an electrical force generated within the body, perhaps through chemical action or the friction of cellular matter, operates upon the mechanical facilities of the body to precipitate their functions. There are sections of the brain which are solely responsible for specific bodily actions, and I have myself activated certain of them by applying electrical currents.'

At first he believed that the application of electrical currents and the resonances it introduced to animal tissue were all that was required in order to reconstitute matter, but was eventually forced to concede that the problem was more than just the identification of the relevant frequencies.

'I have conducted the most exhaustive tests that I have been able to devise but have made no more than a partial progress. I have resolved that there are specific electrical resonances which act vigorously upon some but alas not all tissue and stimulate its growth and organisation in a dramatic fashion. Fibrous nervous tissue reacts most energetically to such stimulation, and will repair damaged portions of itself with alacrity. Other body tissue, however, is altogether immune from electrical effects and I am now of the opinion that other agencies must exist which will harmonise with them separately.'

opposite
An air pump designed by Sir Robert Boyle. Viktor's notes describe the construction of a similar device which he used to test the effect of partial vacuums on electrical current.

Viktor began the search for further natural stimulants by assuming that, as the different classifications of cellular tissue were closely related in both form and

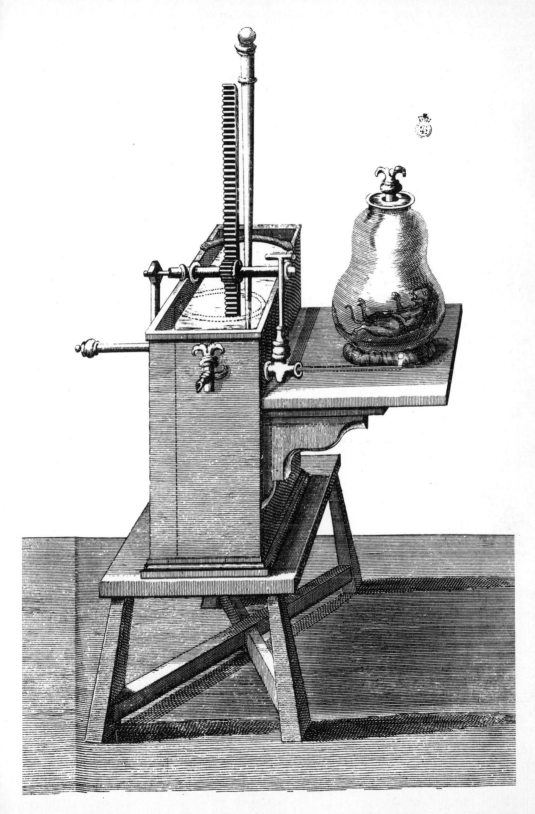

17

composition, the forces he sought must be similarly allied to that of electricity, and he consequently turned to an examination of magnetism. During his many electrical experiments he had often noted effects which were common to both electricity and magnetism and he experimented with electrically produced magnetic fields and their effect on areas of tissue.

'In my initial enthusiasm for this most exciting venture in my scientific career I was foolish enough to assume that I had only to identify one natural force and learn to govern its properties, and the fundamental secrets of life would be revealed to me. Alas that is clearly not the case, but I am not at all downcast at the prospect of further investigation for I have already stumbled upon another governing force. Electrically generated magnetism, though not as potent as its parent force, does certainly act on animal tissue in a beneficial manner and in addition to enhancing the effects of electrical resonance on nervous matter, does manipulate the actions of organic chemical materials in a perceptible manner. I am inspired by a great enthusiasm for at last I am clear as to the direction I must take and can easily contemplate the most tedious labours in the knowledge that I am embarked on an adventure that can be the salvation of mankind and may bestow upon him the freedom of the Earth.'

Despite his exuberance, there followed a long and frustrating period during which his search for other 'Vital Agencies' was unrewarded. He experimented with light and heat as well as with chemical baths and preparations without success, and was beginning to despair when he rediscovered his notes on a series of simple experiments conducted during his first year at the university. One of these had been an examination into the properties of sound, and had been proposed by M. Waldman as an exercise in systematic research to instruct the pupil in the skills required for proper scientific analysis. Frankenstein had produced an essay to summarise his findings, and on re-reading the text, one brief paragraph in his final summary provided him with a vital clue:

'In considering music as the organisation of specific and controllable sonic frequencies, it is interesting to speculate as to what quality in the presentation of a musical work excites in the listener a predictable response. The purely mechanical phenomenon of transmission and reception of audible vibrations does not explain the fact that emotional response is fairly uniform and can be anticipated. Perhaps the seat of emotion possesses certain mechanical properties which are activated by a sympathetic "tuning fork" principle. The sonic vibrations themselves would thus appear to be scarcely less tangible than any other energetic device in the employ of science or industry.'

Viktor seized upon this idea and wrote the following entry on October 2nd.

'I am swept up in a positive frenzy of labour, for I grow daily more certain that I have isolated one more constituent in the pattern of vital energy. I have now succeeded in producing sonic vibrations of extremely high pitch which though undetectable by my ear, do excite a sympathetic resonance in various test materials in a manner similar to that of both electricity and magnetism.

October 7th

There is an entire spectrum of inaudible frequencies which I term "Ethereal Sound"* and several tonal groups within the Ethereal register evoke in me quite categorical emotional responses ranging from maudlin sentiment through elation to a powerful disquiet and incipient fear. My findings are reinforced by the fact that I have elicited identical responses in canine subjects. On subjecting organic tissue samples to the various stimuli of the Ethereal register I found similar changes in growth and reproduction patterns as produced in nervous tissue by the application of electrical stimuli. I have now identified three primary sources of vital influence and consider that my work must now be the study of the effects achieved by various permutations of these three elements on living matter.'

This phrase, and Frankenstein's work in this area, are paralleled by the modern study of Ultrasonics.

Frankenstein hardly left his laboratory at all during the next few weeks, and worked with no regard for the passage of time, sleeping and eating only as he was forced to. He had long been regarded as something of an oddity by both staff and students at the university and was scarcely noticed any more, but this most recent spate of activity began to attract attention as night after night the windows of the isolated laboratory flickered with the cold blue flashes of electrical discharges and darting shadows. Strange sounds echoed in the empty courtyards, and others at the university began to refer to him as 'the Alchemist'. The senior staff, previously content to leave him to his own devices, began to resent his presence and lack of participation in the more usual university activities. M. Waldman, as his official tutor, was increasingly called upon to defend the special status of his pupil until he too began to feel concern.

His attempts to meet with Frankenstein were repeatedly rebuffed and his invitations for informal discussions were never accepted. Eventually the Directors of the university demanded that he offer some justification for Viktor's special status on the grounds that he did not appear to be producing any results of

overleaf
Anatomical studies made during dissections performed as a student at the university.

Zweiter Akt:

Freilegung und Durchsägung
des Patella
Indem die Patella immer weiter
nach oben gedrängt wird,
werden die seitlich von dem
Patellarband gelegenen
Ausstrahlungen des Streckapparates
angespannt und durchtrennt

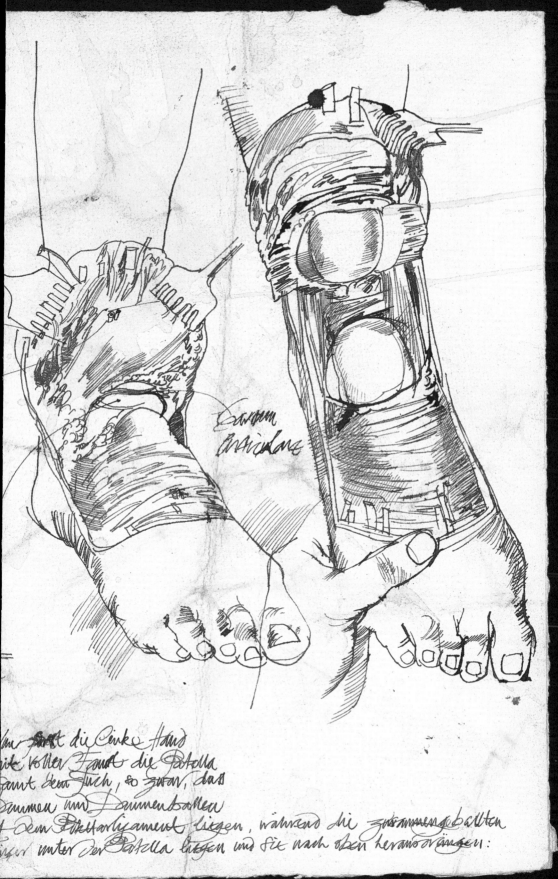

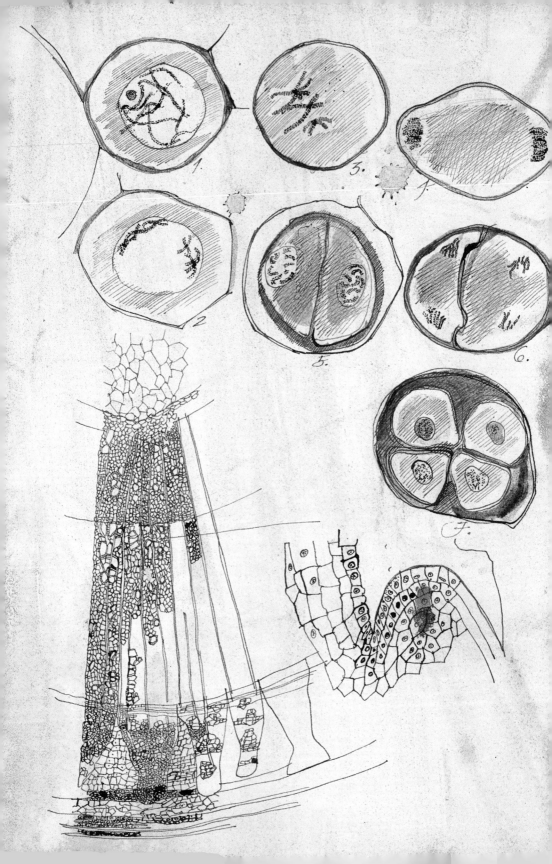

importance. M. Waldman was forced to make a written demand to Frankenstein for an explanation of his activities that would convince the Directors that he should be allowed to continue his private studies within the university.

Viktor Frankenstein knew only too well what the reaction of his scientific colleagues to his convictions and work could be, should they become known. The thought that his quest might be forcibly terminated by 'blind prejudice and the acolytes of superstition' began to obsess him, and he worked in an increasingly hysterical frenzy, refused to communicate with anyone and conducted his formidable programme of research in the utmost secrecy. He equipped the university laboratory allowed to him with an elaborate system of locks, and had the windows fitted with shutters.

His virtual disappearance aroused Waldman's concern about his state of health, but his attempts to make contact with Viktor only served to heighten the latter's paranoia.

November 24th

'I fear that the forces of mischief are marshalling, perhaps at the behest of Satan himself, for who else would be so concerned lest Man opens the door to the reality of God, and shows his truth to the world. Even gentle Waldman has turned against me, and plagues me with prying notes and insidious enquiries. I have written to him to state that I am at a critical juncture in an important series of studies, and that I must be allowed to continue undisturbed for the present. I will then make full report of my activities to the appropriate authorities. I trust that they will be satisfied enough by this to leave me alone a little while longer.

November 27th

All through medical history Man has attempted to define the Vital Force by all manner of means, but he has lacked facilities for establishing a starting place from which to examine its properties. I am convinced that we now have the key, for through our growing knowledge of electricity we are learning ways of investigating phenomena which are neither solid material, nor gaseous, nor yet liquid. This force must be represented by another realm of qualities such as those of electricity, magnetism and Ethereal Sound. Boyle's *Origins of Forms and Qualities* proposes that life is the result of two primary qualities, motion and matter, and that God-given motion instills into the fundamental particles of matter the movements and relationships that determine the development

opposite
As part of his work at Ingolstadt, Viktor painstakingly recorded his observations through the microscope. Those shown here are notable for the accuracy with which he recorded cellular structure and the process of reproduction by division.

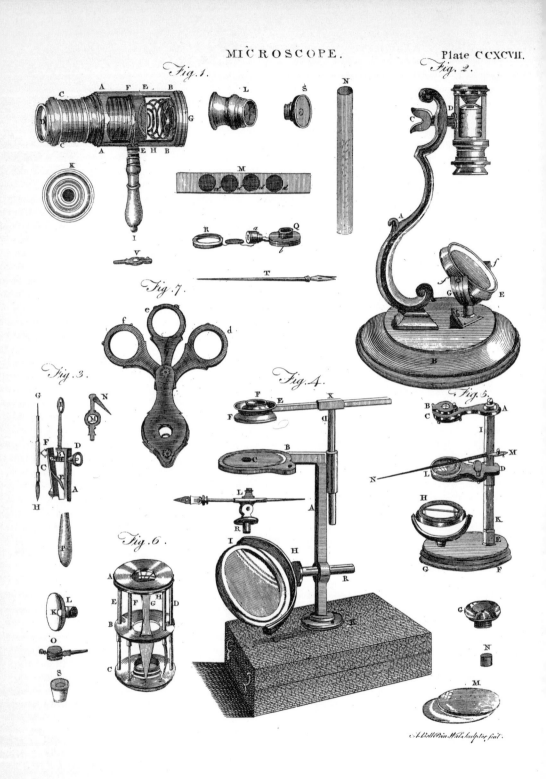

As Frankenstein's studies at Ingolstadt progressed, he began to concentrate on the examination of biological tissue. Shown here are various types of microscope that were in common use at this time.

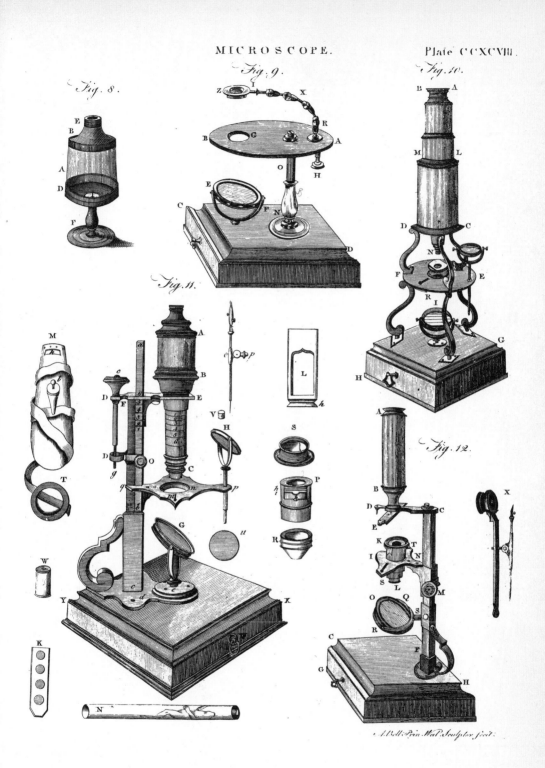

Fig. 8. Fig. 9. Fig. 10. Fig. 11. Fig. 12.

A.Bell Prin. Wal. Sculptor fecit.

25

and nature of all materials, whether living or inanimate. I believe that this Prime Motion either is, or can be simulated by a combination of the three Ethereal properties I have been experimenting with. I have already demonstrated to my own satisfaction that the growth of cellular plant material can be significantly accelerated by the application of influences produced by these three agencies. My chief concern now is to achieve a complete examination of my hypothesis before time cheats me of a fulfilment of my quest. I believe that I have stumbled upon the greatest revelation since Adam ate of the Apple of Wisdom, but there is a great journey to be made before the truth is revealed in all its majesty. God grant me strength.

December 20th

A man can do no more in the search for truth than strive to apply the principles of reason and logic to the mysteries he seeks to resolve, and to pursue his course with industry and application. But however well-formed

his deductions, however energetic his endeavours, all effort is shamed by the brilliant, accidental spark of inspiration. Whether that humbling event appears from within as intuition, or from without as divine coincidence is immaterial to its effect. It is only important that it does occur.

Uncertain as to how I should proceed in my researches, I spent several hours during the early part of the day in idly experimenting with various combinations of the three agencies; altering the frequency of Ethereal Sound produced by my equipment with various magnitudes of electrical and magnetic stimulation. The subject was a sample dish containing several examples of the unicellular organism, Amoeba. Although, from my close observation of its habits, I am particularly familiar with its rate of mitosis under varying conditions, it was some time before I noticed a remarkable increase in the reproductive rate of the sample before me. The speed with which cell-division was taking place was certainly extraordinary, but the phenomenon which seized my attention, with such ferocity that my heart stood still, was the recommencement of activity in examples that

This sketch was probably made at Ingolstadt during Viktor's experiments in electrical stimulation. It shows the brain of a dog into which various electrodes have been introduced.

had certainly died. I could not credit my observations, and worked into the night to check and re-check the experiment until I could not deny the miracle that was taking place before my eyes. Even if examples were destroyed by removing them from their watery environment, once replaced and subjected to the stimulations of the apparatus they reconstituted themselves and began to reproduce with increasing rapidity. God has rewarded my dedication and led me on to the path He must wish me to tread.

December 28th

My physical reserves threaten to fail me at the point when I have most need of strength and vigour. I have worked unceasingly since the revelation, recording the nuances of vital stimulation and their various degrees of effectiveness with meticulous precision. I have also applied the process to other forms of plant and animal tissue, with equally dramatic results, and am now certain that I have stumbled on a fundamental principle of the spontaneous generation of life. God is at my elbow, and urges me onwards, but I can sense that there are other more sinister forces at hand. If God is indeed instrumental in this great study, then there is one who will surely resent my success, and I fear lest his intervention is encouraged.

December 31st

Satan has indeed entered the lists, and I am as helpless in this interplay of forces as an insect in the midst of a fearsome storm. Innocent of the coming conflict, I had progressed my studies to the point where I could undertake to apply my techniques to a human foetus, and had, by clandestine means, obtained a subject that had expired less than an hour earlier, after little more than ten weeks in the womb. Working as speedily as care would permit, I introduced a flow of blood to the tiny cadaver. The blood passed through a device which introduced air and removed the impure vapours, and I simultaneously subjected the foetus to the stimulus of the three agencies. Hours passed without detectable response. The enforced inactivity allowed me to fall victim to my exhaustion, and I confess that I slept. When I awoke, it was with alarm at my carelessness, and I leapt to my feet and rushed to the table and the tangle of filaments that surrounded the subject. It was hideous. The small corpse had doubled in size, its form vanished in a shapeless sprawl of spongy, translucent tissue that seemed to glow with a loathesome inner light as the tangled network of blood vessels bulged and twitched

with the movement of the ichor within their walls. Nothing remotely human lay in the swollen, gelatinous thing that pulsed moistly before me. Horror welled up from the dark caverns of my mind and a silent scream of disgust and fear echoed shrilly in my inner ear. As I stared, structures within it began to break down, spilling their obscene contents out into the trembling bag of skin. Unable to control my utter revulsion, I clutched at the table, overturning it and hurling the object to the floor, where it burst wetly. I seized the lamp, dashed it to the ground and staggered from the room as the flames erupted behind me. Even as I write, the vision of that dreadful form keeps impinging on my vision and strange sounds fill the chamber.'

Viktor's first experiment in the artificial stimulation of lifeless human tissue was a ghastly failure, as his drawing of this grotesquely overblown foetus demonstrates. The horror this result inspired in him caused a complete nervous collapse and, later, abandonment of his studies.

The Christmas Viktor had promised to spend with his family had come and gone unnoticed by him, and letters from his father lay unopened on the floor. His biography might have ended there but for the tradesman he had instructed to deliver food to his rooms. When the latter found that the prevous week's supply had remained uncollected outside the door he had the initiative to inform the landlord, who on investigation reported to the university that Viktor was apparently ill. After several attempts to communicate with him, college porters eventually broke down the door.

The letter sent to Wilhelm Frankenstein by the dean of the university provides a vivid impression of the scene which met their eyes.

'Upon breaching your son's rooms, the staff were assailed by a repugnant odour, and it was clear that he had not vacated his rooms for any reason for several days. Everything was in great disorder. Your son was found to be crouched, wrapped in a fouled blanket, in the furthest corner of the room, and although conscious, did not appear to be aware of our entry, but was staring wildly about in a most alarming fashion. He was transported with the very greatest difficulty to the Infirmary, where he remains at present.

'We have taken the liberty of calling upon the services of a local physician well versed in such mental disabilities as are exhibited by your son, and he has indicated that your son's illness is grave, but that prompt attention should allow a cure to be effected. We shall not, of course, make any provision until we receive your authority.'

The letter was transmitted by hand, but as the family were away, the housekeeper directed them to the house of an old family friend, M. Clerval, who opened the letter. In view of the gravity of the matter, his son Henri Clerval, Viktor's closest childhood friend, was dispatched to Ingolstadt. It was a fortunate action, for as the horrified Henri stared at the emaciated face of his old friend, Viktor's anguished face relaxed at once. Viktor wrote later: 'If dear Henri had not rescued me from that bed, I should, without doubt, have ended my days incarcerated in some dismal cell, my mind forever consumed in hellish visions'. Despite the immediate improvement in his manner, however, the agony was far from over.

A Fateful
Interlude

Pending the return of Viktor's father, and in view of his
friend's willingness to co-operate with him, Henri was
permitted to return with the patient to the lodging house,
now cleaned and aired. Although the attending physician
made regular visits, the outward improvement in Viktor's
condition was obviously due to the continuing presence
of Henri, who was most conscientious in persuading
Viktor to adhere to a proper diet, attend to personal
hygiene, and to take exercise. Wilhelm Frankenstein
visited them on several occasions and was sufficiently
impressed by his son's progress to reject the idea of
having him committed to an asylum. A letter from him to
Henri demonstrates his optimism.

'I count myself and Viktor most fortunate in having so
stalwart and selfless an ally in our plight. I do not know
what course I would otherwise have followed, as my
understanding of my son's extraordinary intellect
convinces me that conventional treatment would have
meant life-long incarceration. I have a profound respect
for physicians, but their science is for ordinary men, and
I am certain that they would, quite reasonably, interpret
Viktor's unusual intellectual processes as continuing
evidence of his ill health. I cannot help but believe that
his contagion is that of excessive solitude, and that I
cannot provide the companionship he requires so
urgently, being neither a scientist of equal stature nor a
brother in years. Though you, dear Henri, are by your
own admission not the former, you are assuredly the
latter and much loved by him. I have discussed the
situation with your father, and he is quite happy for you to
continue residing in Ingolstadt for as long as you feel
willing.'

Viktor's physical well-being was quite easily and
swiftly restored, but the distress suffered by his mind was
slow to repair. For several weeks he was only able to
sleep with the assistance of sedatives, and even then his
nights were fitful, punctuated by bouts of waking terror
during which he had to be forcibly restrained by the
faithful Henri. But gradually his periods of calmness and
lucidity grew more prolonged, and he took pleasure from
walking about the town with Henri. After three months
had passed, he once again began recording the day's
events in his diaries, which he kept entirely to himself,
but he never alluded to his former activities, and appeared
to have dismissed them from his thoughts altogether. He
began to throw himself into life with a hedonistic fury that

Henri Clerval was the son of one of Wilhelm Frankenstein's oldest friends and had been associated with the family throughout his childhood. When Viktor fell seriously ill at Ingolstadt, he volunteered to attend upon him and eventually succeeded in bringing him back to Geneva. He was an accomplished artist, and there is reason to believe that the painting is a self-portrait.

startled even the lively Henri, roistering and debauching his way through the nights and the substantial funds furnished by his father. Henri became concerned as it seemed only a matter of time before Viktor's excesses either returned him to the state of exhaustion from which he had so recently recovered, or led him into a serious scandal. He had already incurred the disfavour of several notable families as a result of the attentions he pressed on their daughters, and had been involved in a number of unpleasant incidents in some of the local hostelries.

His debts had also begun to mount and one morning Henri, deciding that he must act in his friend's best interest, hired a carriage, heaved the totally inebriated Viktor aboard and was half-way back to the family home before the latter awoke.

It was over three years since Viktor had set foot in the house, and after a few difficult days the familiar surroundings and affectionate concern of his father and

Wilhelm Frankenstein, Viktor's father, was a highly respected member of the Genevese legal fraternity. He was, however, the last in a long line of lawyers and magistrates as, apart from Viktor's brief involvement in practice, none of his sons carried on the tradition.

brothers had a profound effect. His youngest brother, William, was almost a stranger to him, but they were soon devoted to each other, Viktor taking great delight in teaching and entertaining him. Throughout the next year, his father made several attempts to encourage Viktor in considering a return to his studies, but the latter refused steadfastly to be drawn into any discussion of his earlier life. He professed an interest in participating in his father's law practice and began to study the subject. It was then that he was introduced to one of his father's colleagues and his daughter, Elizabeth Lavenza.

December 26th

'What a day of enchantment this has been. I awoke this morning feeling no great enthusiasm for the day ahead, as my father intended to entertain large numbers of his

The Frankensteins' Geneva home fell into disrepair soon after the death of Ernest Frankenstein. This photograph was taken in 1890, shortly before it was demolished.

acquaintances and clients and I do not enjoy such occasions. Nevertheless, I felt bound to participate in the endless round of toasts and empty chatter, and resigned myself to a tedious day. All was much as I had anticipated until the afternoon, when more callers appeared as soon as we had taken lunch. As the party entered the drawing room, and I prepared myself for another round of gentle speeches, I found myself fixed to the spot and staring in a most unseemly fashion at the creature that accompanied my father's friends. She was a vision of such delight that I was robbed of speech, and could only stammer idiotically when we were introduced. It was a most extraordinary sensation, for at once my tongue fastened itself to the roof of my mouth and would not translate my thoughts into words. I dared not even move lest I blunder clumsily against the furniture. As we faced one another, I felt my cheeks flush with embarrassment at my predicament. But how perfect she was, for she perceived my discomfiture directly, and strove at once to put me at my ease. Her manner was warm and she talked as though we had known each other for some time, yet without the slightest suggestion of presumptuousness. Within a few moments I was perfectly myself again, and lost all sense of time as we conversed. Eventually, my father chided me laughingly for keeping her to myself and I felt a painful wrench as he led her to another part of the room.

Though others engaged me in conversation, my glance kept straying to where she stood, and several times our eyes met with a suddenness that stole my breath away. After an hour or so, my father announced that Elizabeth, for that was her name, would play and sing for us, and she consented with a most appealing grace. I gazed at her with undisguised admiration. To my joy, some quality in her eyes as she returned my look allowed me to perceive that she too sensed some magical attraction, and I felt as though a strange and wondrous flower had blossomed within my breast. What agony I felt as the time of her departure arrived, and all gathered at the door to bid their farewells. As she approached me, I took her cape from the servant, and she turned to allow me to place it about her shoulders with a pretty laugh that pierced my heart. I could not bear to see her leave without knowing whether I should see her again, and so, with my heart pounding in fear of a rebuff, I begged leave to call upon her. At that instant, the others approached, and she would not answer, but as they stepped outside she took my hand and squeezed it tightly before skipping lightly down to their carriage. My head whirled and I scarcely knew where I was. Suddenly I could not bear to accompany the rest of the family back into the drawing room and, excusing myself, retired directly to my room. I feel as though I am in the grip of a fever, but know that I am in excellent health. I can think of nothing but Elizabeth, and believe that I must be utterly in love, for I ache at the thought of the time that must pass before I can gaze upon that perfect face again.'

Viktor received an invitation to call upon the Lavenza family a few days later, and before long was a regular visitor to their home. Soon a close attachment had formed between Viktor and Elizabeth, and it became clear to all that they were admirably suited to one another. Elizabeth was as intelligent and inquisitive as she was beautiful, and Viktor found her one of the few people to whom he could open his heart and mind. It was inevitable that they should begin to consider marriage.

March 12th

Today Elizabeth and I shall take William for a picnic. The weather is unusually mild and the rain has ceased at last so it will be a pleasant change for all of us. I think that the time has come for me to speak of marriage between us, for I now play a useful part in father's practice and should be considering the establishment of my own house. Dear

This engraving was discovered among Viktor Frankenstein's papers, and although undocumented, it is probably a representation of his wife, Elizabeth Lavenza. Her mysterious death in his company brought to an end his attempt to return to a more conventional way of life.

Elizabeth has made no mention of it but I am certain that she considers the matter often and would be happy at the prospect. I hope William will not be distressed at my departing the house, but there will be ample time for him to become accustomed to the idea, and he would, I'm sure, find it exciting to have two houses to think of as home. I shall speak with her today if the opportunity arises.

March 13th

I proposed to Elizabeth yesterday. It was a curious event. I felt most peculiarly ill at ease, and suddenly saw her as though she were a stranger. She must have felt the same for she blushed in a most becoming fashion, and could

scarcely utter her consent. We came home directly and told father, who was overjoyed; he is very fond of her. That evening I visited her father to ask his permission, which was most graciously given. We all dined together, and afterwards Elizabeth and her mother vanished to talk of the preparations as though the wedding were to take place at once rather than in the autumn.'

The intervening months passed swiftly and serenely apart from one extraordinary interlude. Wilhelm Frankenstein announced one morning that he had just received a letter from professor Waldman, enquiring as to Viktor's well-being and asking if he might visit the family as he was soon to be passing nearby. Viktor became so pale that his father feared he might faint, then, leaping to his feet, he launched into a furious tirade of invective against his father before storming off and locking himself into his room. When he emerged some hours later he behaved in his usual jovial fashion, as though nothing untoward had taken place, and made no reference to the

The house on Lake Como owned by the Frankenstein family, where Viktor and his wife spent their honeymoon and which was the setting for her tragic death.

matter on any subsequent occasion. His father did not raise the matter again and informed Waldman that for various reasons it would not be convenient.

Eventually the day of the wedding arrived, and the event passed off amid much celebration and festivity, ending with the couple mounting the carriage for the journey to Lake Como, where they were to spend their honeymoon at the house on the shore owned by Viktor's father. They spent the time wandering along the hillside paths or idly drifting on the clear water in the small rowing boat kept there. The days were leisurely and idyllic and in the evenings they huddled before the fire, talking of their plans and of the house that Elizabeth's father had provided for them. But the dark stars that directed Viktor's life were soon to exert their sinister influence once more.

September 22nd

'Our gentle rapture has been cruelly disturbed and the news that my dearest brother William is ill has fallen like a stone into the tranquillity of our hours. Though the messenger was at pains to point out that my father did not feel my presence would be required, I am torn between the strongest sense of fraternal loyalty and my acute reluctance to interrupt our joyous solitude. I know Elizabeth would be most dismayed if she knew of my dilemma, but the enchantment of such a sojourn as this is a fragile thing, and the spell, once broken, can rarely be retrieved. I must conceal my alarm and make no mention of it until I receive further news. Even then I will only appraise her of it should his condition deteriorate. God grant that it should not be so, for I cannot bear the thought that our blissful state should be marred by such unfortunate circumstances.

September 23rd

The old woman who tends the house for us called today with an excellent repast packed in a hamper, and we spent the day rowing idly along the shores of the lake. The weather has been most agreeable, and this day would have been one of the happiest of our stay here, had my mind not been preoccupied with morbid fantasies about my brother's condition. I wish that I had more news of his progress. Elizabeth has noticed my uncertain mood and keeps remarking on it. For some reason I find her anxiety irritating, and in an unguarded moment I admonished her abruptly, though I was instantly ashamed and tried to make amends for the obvious grief I caused her. The sight of her startled face and the tears that brimmed unbidden in her eyes cut me deeply.

September 24th

Still no news of William. Elizabeth appears to have
forgiven me for my unwarranted outburst, but I suspect
that she now believes, albeit reluctantly, that there are
aspects of me that she is not familiar with. I fear that
William's illness has already interfered with us despite
her ignorance of it. We both behaved as usual today, but
there is some tiny shift in our perspectives, and I suspect
that a small piece of magic has been stolen away from us.
I find myself standing at the window quite frequently,
staring down the road along which news will come, while
Elizabeth tries bravely to ignore my silences. I feel a
strange uneasiness and occasionally find myself at once
resentful of the very love that discourages me from
leaving for home at once, and vexed by the fraternal love
that seeks to disrupt our marital harmony. I have become
restless and fractious, and Elizabeth's attempts to
comfort me only serve to aggravate my condition.
Perhaps it is best that we should accept the inevitable and
conclude our holiday at once in order to return to Geneva
and William.'

The events of the following day remain a source of
mystery, for they are not recorded in Viktor's diary, or in
his later writings. The essential facts are found in other
contemporary accounts, such as the local newspaper,
but though the drama is described it is not explained. It
appears that Viktor, having at last informed Elizabeth of
his brother's illness, decided that they should remain one
more day before returning home, and the couple set off
for a last boat trip around the lake. The housekeeper who
came each morning to attend to the domestic tasks
recollected watching them row off round the small point
near the house shortly before lunch. She had been
informed of their intention to leave the next morning, and
had volunteered to remain in order to prepare supper and
assist them in packing their belongings for the journey
back. They had both expressed their gratitude, and had
been in a light-hearted mood as they carried a packed
lunch on to the little craft. By the time it began to grow
dark, however, they had not returned, and the housekeeper became concerned and walked down to the small
jetty to see if they were in sight. Unable to detect any sign
of them, she walked along the shore in the direction they
had taken, having first fetched a lantern in view of the
increasing gloom. By its light she eventually discovered
the soaked and unconscious form of Viktor, lying in the
shallows of a small beach. His face was scratched and
bleeding and his coat was torn. Fearing the worst, the
housekeeper peered into the darkness but there was no
sign of either the boat or Elizabeth, and after trying
unsuccessfully to awaken Viktor, she hastened back to
the nearest house to seek help. While some set out in

William Frankenstein, the youngest of the three brothers, whose untimely death under curious circumstances had a profound effect upon Viktor. There remains in this tragedy some doubt of Viktor's innocence.

their fishing boats, others followed the old lady back to where Viktor now sat, his eyes glazed, rocking quietly to and fro in a peculiar fashion. He showed no awareness of their presence but allowed himself to be led back to the house, while the others continued to search for Elizabeth. Suddenly there was a flurry of activity among the bobbing lanterns, and a few minutes later one of the boats grated over the pebbles of the beach. In it lay the pale, battered body of Elizabeth.

By the next morning, Viktor was physically recovered though distraught with grief. When questioned by the magistrate, he explained that they had been on their way back to the house when a strange and sudden darkness had descended, so dense that he was scarcely able to see his wife as she slept in the stern of the craft. The next instant, the boat seemed to pitch and toss as though in the grip of a squall, despite the lack of wind. He remembered gripping the sides and making his way towards Elizabeth when everything went black. The next thing he was aware of was being led into the warmth of the house, before he once again passed into unconsciousness. Although a party set out that afternoon in order to investigate the spot, no clue to the cause of the tragedy could be found. Viktor sat with Elizabeth's body throughout the day, and was only persuaded to retire to bed with the greatest difficulty. The next day he rose early, and made arrangements to return at once with the body to Geneva.

September 27th

'In all my unhappy life, I could never have imagined such misery as I am now suffering. My precious Elizabeth has been torn from me and my heart bleeds with a wound that will never heal. How can this terrible tragedy have come to pass? Why, dear God, why have I been stricken with this mortal blow, for I cannot conceive of life without her sweetness and gentle beauty. We had only just planted the seed of a flower whose blooms would have glowed in our lives like a lantern, yet its first trembling shoot has been ground most cruelly into the eternal dust by the malevolent heel of a bitter destiny. I am bewildered and lost in a huge void of silent misery, my lonely cries snatched from my lips and hurled away in tattered fragments by the shrieking wind of despair. Elizabeth, answer me Elizabeth! I wander through the gale-scoured landscape in pursuit of visions that skim the horizon like bedraggled clouds. I see William, lying pale and fevered, his eyes staring blindly into the black skies overhead. Somehow he is part of the cosmic game that has claimed my love. His eyes see into the dark mists of eternity and watch her playing among the fields of Elysium, where I cannot tread. Why is he permitted the glimpse that I myself would willingly die for? Why is he preparing for a hallowed journey that is forbidden to me? William, what part have you in this timeless play?'

A few days later, William too had died. Though fatally ill with tuberculosis, his death came suddenly enough to surprise the doctors attending him, and though there was no evidence of a pulmonary blockage, it was clear that he had suffocated during the night. Despite the great disorder of William's bedding, Viktor, whose room lay opposite, had heard nothing of his brother's violent death throes. Although all had resigned themselves to the outcome of William's illness, none was prepared for the abruptness with which it had occurred. This second tragedy proved more than Viktor could bear, and for two days he remained locked in his room, refusing to accept food or to communicate. Then, without a word to anyone, he emerged with a small valise, descended the stairs and left the house. It was the last his father ever saw of him.

The Quest Begins

The tragic death of his wife and the further loss of William brought to an abrupt end Viktor's attempt to live an ordinary life, and set him on the path of the last and strangest period of his extraordinary history. Unexpectedly, his diaries reflect none of the acute melancholia into which he was plunged by earlier sorrows, such as the loss of his mother, but rather demonstrate a quiet resignation and resolve.

August 9th

My great intelligence and its demands on my attentions have always set me apart from my fellow men. In every age there are some who are called to pursue a destiny, who are given life in order to be the instrument through which a divine purpose is accomplished, and they are not heirs to the rights of ordinary mortals. From my childhood I have sensed that I was destined to fulfill some great purpose, and I am convicted that every aspect of my existence has been designed to prepare me for my future role. Now that I have been so harshly separated from life, and all associations so abruptly shorn away, I believe the day of my true destiny to be dawning. My humanity is behind me and I am prepared for battle.

August 11th

I cannot bear to contemplate the resumption of my work within society's bounds, and must seek a refuge where I might pursue my goals undisturbed by the company of men. As I deliberated upon the question, I recalled the existence of our ancient ancestral home, and have sought the complicity of my brother Ernest in secretly furnishing me with some of the family documents relating to it. From these I have determined that although the lands have long since passed from us by default, the pile itself, being much abused by time and the elements, has not been similarly appropriated. According to a letter from my great-grandfather to his wife, written whilst touring the country, he took the opportunity to visit the old castle, reporting that although it was in very poor repair, much was reasonably well preserved. I am excited by the possibility that it may prove habitable, and am determined to make my way there in exploration, for no better setting could I imagine for my studies; isolated yet already part of my heritage. Although I do not know its precise location, I shall set out forthwith to find and examine it.

August 30th

How many times during the last three weeks have I despaired of finding the castle, yet something convinced me to persist in my search. Now at last the routine of investigating local records, interrogating the inhabitants of lonely villages and perusing maps of the region is at an end. It was with a sense of weary resignation that I entered this last dreary hamlet and made my way to the local magistrate's office, but my feelings changed swiftly to those of exultation, for at last my quest is over, and the site of Schwarzstein castle discovered. I gave the magistrate no intimation of my true purpose, saying only that I had come to take up residence in the old family home, and though he seemed bemused and expressed concern at my apparent ignorance of its dilapidation, he

High above the gloomy forests of Schwarzstein towered the long-deserted and derelict castle of the Frankenstein family. It was here that Viktor returned to complete the work that had occupied him for the greater part of his life, and which was to become the setting for the horrors which followed.

was content to direct me to it. I set out at once, on foot as he assured me that it lay not two miles from the town, and made my way upwards through a dense and gloomy forest that seemed interminable. I eventually found a little-used track winding up among the ragged outcrops of rock that became increasingly in evidence, until I breasted a steep incline where I paused to catch my breath. As I leaned against a rough shoulder of rock, I looked about me and suddenly beheld the object of my search.

The castle stood stark against the sky, appearing only as a harsh, black outline deserving of its name, its battlements like the scaly back of some ancient monster. Filled with the vigour of excitement, I set off briskly towards it, and was soon approaching the gates. It seemed to tower above me, filling the sky. Despite my enthusiasm, I could not help but observe that time had indeed mistreated it. Grasses and ferns grew among the moist stone of its flanks, and the sky was visible through many of the upper windows. The ground beneath the walls was littered with fragments of collapsed masonry, and I began to suspect that my journey had been wasted. Brambles and scrubby growth obstructed the dark gateway, but I eventually found myself before the rotting remains of the heavy wooden doors, which were held together only by their rusted ironwork and hinges. One was ajar, and I entered, warily eyeing the crumbling stonework above. The courtyard was much overgrown, the flags cracked and disturbed by the roots of the shrubs and saplings that grew in wild profusion, and I was startled by the sudden flight of the wild goats that grazed there. Beyond the courtyard loomed the black, mossy walls of the main keep and living apartments, and I directed my steps there in a dispirited fashion. As I drew closer, however, my confidence increased, for the edifice was of such massive construction that it appeared to be in reasonable order. One wing, of more fragile form, was certainly beyond repair, and the roof of that quarter had collapsed entirely, but the greater part was more stoutly made. I entered through the debris of the original door to find the dim interior quite sound and dry. A massive stone stairway ascended via a carved granite gallery to the upper apartments, and I climbed cautiously up to find them in good condition, the floors being also of granite slabs. The floor above that was similarly well preserved, although some shallow pools of water attested to the incompleteness of the roof.

As I peered from one of the windows into the courtyard far below, I was seized with a joyous resolution. This was indeed the solution to my dilemma, and the strange sensation that my presence here had been ordained swept over me. It seemed as though I had always known this empty place; each room I entered seemed familiar. I wandered about absorbed in my plans, and scarcely

An old map of Germany showing the position of Schwarzstein in northern Bavaria (Franconia).

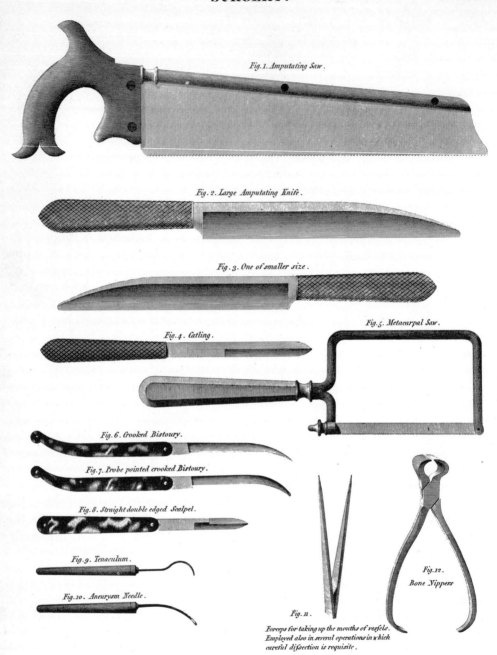

Fig. 1. Amputating Saw.

Fig. 2. Large Amputating Knife.

Fig. 3. One of smaller size.

Fig. 4. Catling.

Fig. 5. Metacarpal Saw.

Fig. 6. Crooked Bistoury.

Fig. 7. Probe pointed crooked Bistoury.

Fig. 8. Straight double edged Scalpel.

Fig. 9. Tenaculum.

Fig. 10. Aneurysm Needle.

Fig. 11.
Forceps for taking up the mouths of vessels.
Employed also in several operations in which
careful dissection is requisite.

Fig. 12.
Bone Nippers

*A selection of surgical
instruments and appliances
typical of those employed by
Viktor in his studies.*

Plate CCCCXCI.

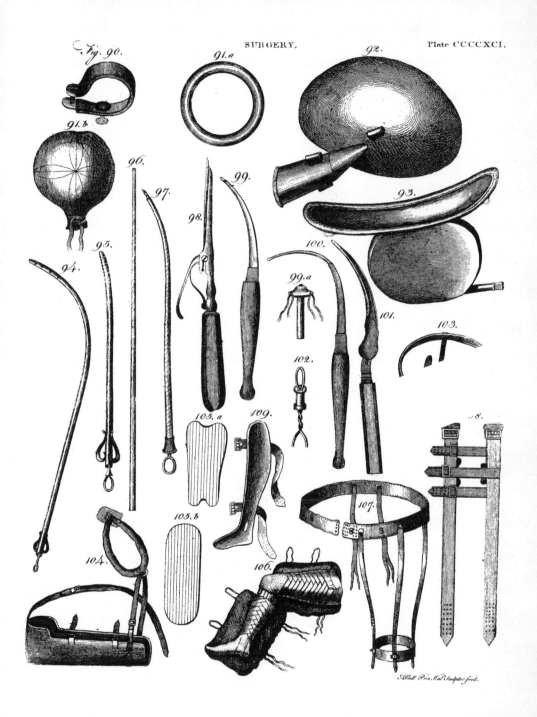

Fig. 90. 91.a 92. 91.b 96. 97. 99. 98. 95. 100. 93. 99.a 94. 101. 103. 102. 105.a 109. 108. 107. 105.b 104. 106.

A.Bell Prin.Wal.Sculptor fecit.

noticed the passage of time until the gathering dusk made it impossible to explore further. I had stayed too long, and knew that I would lose my way should I attempt to return through the labyrinthine wood in the dark, so I resolved to spend my first night in my new-found home, and gathering a quantity of dead bracken, prepared a rude bed in the driest of the upper chambers, where I passed the night deep in contemplation.

August 31st

I arose as soon as the room began to lighten, having slept little, and after a last tour of the ancient building set off at a brisk pace through the desolate woods to the town below. There I took a room in the local inn and began to lay my plans for the occupation of the family seat. Later in the day, I returned with a party of slightly suspicious artisans to survey the castle and to determine precisely what had to be done to restore at least a portion of the edifice sufficiently to provide a degree of comfort and security. There is much to be done, but I am confident that it will not be long before I am ensconced there. I shall stay here a few days to make arrangements for the work to be initiated, then must return to Ingolstadt to prepare for my removal to this place. I have financial arrangements to make in addition to collecting the papers and equipment that remain at Ingolstadt. Once these matters have been attended to, I shall return to watch over the refurbishment and prepare for the resumption of my studies.

November 12th

The village has been able to provide ample labour for the restoration of the buildings. There is too much decay for the work to furnish anything more than the most rudimentary comforts, but they will at least be adequate. Work progresses quickly and my living quarters are already prepared and furnished. I have determined where the laboratory shall be made, and as soon as it has been cleared and made fast against the elements, I shall dispense with the men. I bitterly resent the delay in the joining of battle. Death the Plunderer is abroad in the world, and each day that passes is witness to his foul thieving from the estate of Man.

November 29th

My solitude is now complete. The men have left, and I have worked hard these last few days to unpack my equipment and move it to the laboratory. It is no match

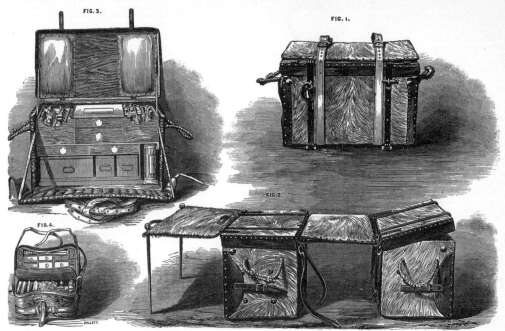

FIG. 3.

FIG. 1.

FIG. 2.

FIG. 4.

FIG 1. MEDICINE PANNIER PACKED FOR TRAVELLING. 2. TWO MEDICINE PANNIERS FORMING AN OPERATING-TABLE. 3. MEDICINE PANNIER OPEN. 4. MEDICAL FIELD COMPANION.

BRITISH MEDICINE PANNIERS,—SEE PAGE 247.

for the facilities I enjoyed at Ingolstadt, but I shall make it one of the most advanced study rooms of my time once everything has arrived. My books, so long neglected, live again as I turn the pages to refresh my knowledge. My recent life seems but a fantastic dream and I can scarcely credit it. I was foolish to believe that such an existence could really be mine. In quiet moments I still feel the small stirrings of fear that I experienced during the later days at Ingolstadt, but my resolution dismisses them easily, and I am content to accept the duty I am charged with. God is the spirit of Man free from death, and that is our heritage. All the threads of invention shall be drawn together in me and, once freed from the thongs of mortality, Man shall be at liberty to walk with God upon the Earth. I pray for His strength and guidance in the coming days.

Viktor is known to have possessed a number of portable medical cases which accompanied him to Schwarzstein. The examples shown here are of British design, but his own were probably of very similar construction.

December 21st

Last night I realised that I am in need of assistance, for there are many tasks to be undertaken which require additional hands. I ventured into the town, much against my inclination, in order to seek assistance, and spoke with the Mayor. I suggested only that I was engaged in scientific work of an experimental nature, giving no

overleaf
Frankenstein's plan of the new laboratory he set up in the castle, together with a view of his generating equipment and details of some of the apparatus. The primary drive belt passes through the roof to connect with a windmill.

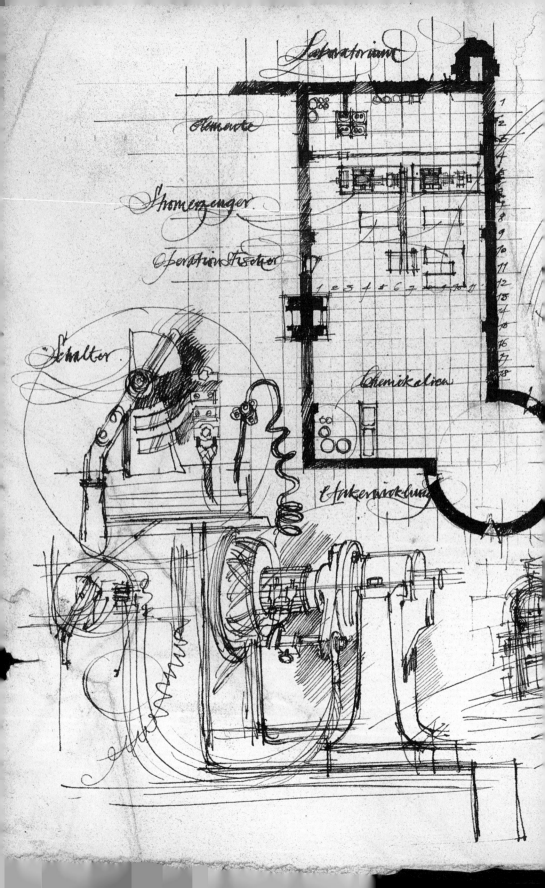

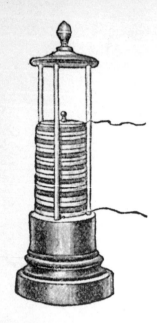

The Voltaic Pile was the earliest known form of battery and played a fundamental part in Viktor Frankenstein's work, though he later perfected superior equipment.

description of it in detail, but I could hardly credit the grotesque ignorance of these people. Science is an anathema to them, and it is clear that they consider such activity to be tantamount to witchcraft! His manner became almost insolent and I retired no nearer the solution to my difficulty. I repaired to the small inn nearby for some refreshment before returning to the castle, and repeated my enquiry in the less formal surroundings there. That too proving fruitless I returned to consider some other course.

December 24th

I have found my accomplice, or rather, he found me. I was staring morosely from my window at the distant lights of the town when I noticed furtive movements amongst the shadows of the woods beneath the walls, and discerned the dark shape of some person scurrying in a peculiar fashion towards the gates. Perplexed, I went down and opened them, but there was no answer to my call. As I was poised to close them once more, a dark and crooked human shape darted past me into the courtyard. Whether beggar or villain, he was of the most unpleasant appearance, scrofulous and of sickly colour, with a gross spinal deformity that looked to be result of some terrible accident rather than of a congenital disorder. He made no answer to my questioning, but his mouthings and the guttural sounds he emitted made it plain that he did not possess the power of speech, so I indicated that he should follow me to my makeshift kitchen, where I made him some broth. He consumed it with unseemly haste, watching me all the while as though afraid I would turn on him. I then led him to a place where he could sleep, taking great care that he could not enter my own apartments during the night.

I shall talk to him tomorrow, and see if I can persuade him to enter my service, as he could not be better suited to my needs. Though in sore need of a regular diet and rest, he is powerfully built and agile, while his inability to speak is to my advantage, as I have no wish to have my affairs broadcast to the world at large. I will try to learn more of him tomorrow.

December 25th

The new member of my household is something of a kinsman, being also an outcast among men. Ascertaining his story proved a lengthy procedure due to his dumbness, but by dint of careful questioning and explicit gestures we communicated after a fashion. As I suspected, his deformities are not due to natural causes, but are the result of an unsuccessful attempt at hanging. His

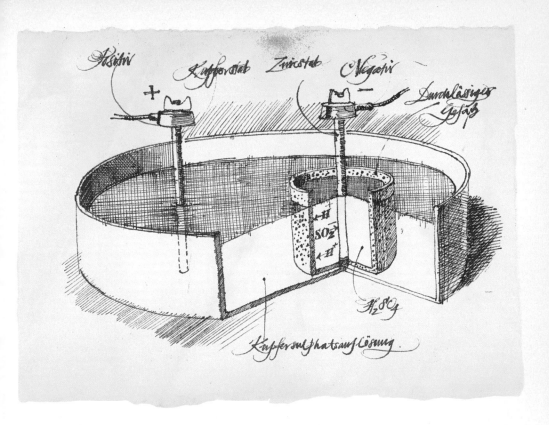

Much of Frankenstein's work in the field of electrical research was far in advance of current studies. This diagram of a battery shows that he was already working with apparatus that was not officially 'invented' until much later.

spine was severely dislocated and his larynx crushed, but he miraculously survived. I questioned him as to the reasons for his punishment, but he would not admit to having perpetrated any crime. I am inclined to believe that, as a simpleton and vagabond, he was indeed made a scapegoat for some local scandal. It is easy to understand such an attitude in view of his quite exceptional unattractiveness. Even leaving aside his deformity, he seems scarcely human, being ill-made in other respects. Although not actually a dwarf, he displays similar characteristics, being unnaturally short in the legs, which are bowed as though from ricketts. His black, thick hair, swarthy features and pronounced cheekbones suggest Slavic origins. How he has lived for as many years as he suggests in these inhospitable woods, I do not know, but he seems delighted with the prospect of working in my employ, and has showed no interest in enquiring as to his duties. He was of great use in assisting me with the removal of my equipment to the new laboratory. I think he will suit me admirably.

December 29th

One of the consignments from London arrived today and I unpacked it with the help of Igor; the name is my own as he was never given one. The cases mainly contained chemicals, so I can at last carry out some of the experimental work I have been so impatient to start. Electricity plays a vital role in the work I intend, but the Voltaic Pile is an inferior device for its production, and I intend to improve upon it. The weakness of Alessandro Volta's device is that hydrogen is attracted to the negative plate and progressively reduces the amount of current produced. I believe that if the zinc rod is placed in a porous container of diluted sulphuric acid, the hydrogen released will react with a solution of copper-sulphate to form copper, which will be deposited without harm on the copper electrode. Stability of output will then be assured.*

* This form of battery was officially credited to John Daniell several years later in 1836.

January 8th

I did not awake until nine o'clock this morning, having worked much of the night. More equipment has arrived and the laboratory now has everything I require. My theory of atomic excitation is workable, at least to some degree, as my experiments with plant matter show very positive results. Cellular regeneration is accelerated dramatically through electro-sonic excitation; the rate of cell division has been enhanced threefold in the test samples. It is possible that matter in its smallest part possesses active fields or auras which can be electrically manipulated. The difficulty lies in altering them enough to enhance their inherent properties without distorting their original form. I have reached the most exciting stage of my work, and can forsake my dusty tomes for the tangible reality of practical experiment. My next obstacle is that of procuring specimens for my anatomical studies. I can scarcely approach the officers of the town as it would confirm their visions of me as some satanic ghoul or wizard. I am in the same position as the men of science in past ages who were forced to act outside the law in order to determine medical truths. I have no alternative but to enlist the assistance of poor Igor in the procurement of suitable material.

January 12th

The deed is done! Igor is a 'bodysnatcher' of the highest order and has secured an excellent corpse, which I shall work on directly. I must also order a substantial supply of ice. This place is primitive enough without adding to it the odour of corruption. But I must consider a means of ensuring an adequate supply of corpses, for I cannot rely on the townsfolk to perish at the appropriate times, nor on Igor to be always undetected in his grisly labours. There is a college of medicine at Wurzburg, and perhaps I can reach an agreement with the governors. I am anxious not to draw attention to my works but I see no real alternative.

February 26th

I have all my equipment functioning as it should, and although the setting is a trifle bizarre, I am confident that my laboratory is one of the most advanced in the world. My system for the production of electrical power has proved a great success, and I am poised for the next stage of my work. Professor Waldman has been most generous in his letter of recommendation to the college at Wurzburg, and as the principal of the college is an old acquaintance of his, I foresee no impediment to my securing the material I require. Igor has been of considerable service in assisting me to adapt the carriage for more macabre use. He will leave for Wurzburg tomorrow, and I have impressed on him the absolute need for him to plan the return journey to allow a nocturnal passage through the town, for should any of the stupid inhabitants glimpse its contents, their suspicions of me will be given substance. Meanwhile I shall complete the arrangements for storage of the cadavers.

March 1st

Igor has returned, and I believe he discharged his strange duty with relish. He is of an uncommon disposition. Of the four specimens he delivered, two are superb. and I shall begin surgery directly. Both cadavers are already accepting my plasma preparation through gravity-feed mechanisms, and the solutions are being aerated by the device I have designed to introduce oxygen and extract the carbon-dioxide from the circulated plasma. In a few hours I shall be able to commence the generation of the appropriate auras in order to stimulate cellular potential. I am nervous with excitement as my labours approach the final judgement.

March 14th

I am inordinately tired, having laboured almost without cease these last few days. Something is amiss, and I am not confident of the outcome. I am sure that my theory of physical activity being governed by a spectrum of electro-magnetic influence is correct, but I am uncertain of my identification of the many differing frequencies which govern the body's diverse parts. The subject of my efforts is not responding well. I have attempted to make of the

overleaf
Pre-operative drawings locating the principal areas for constructional surgery, with details of the relevant musculature.

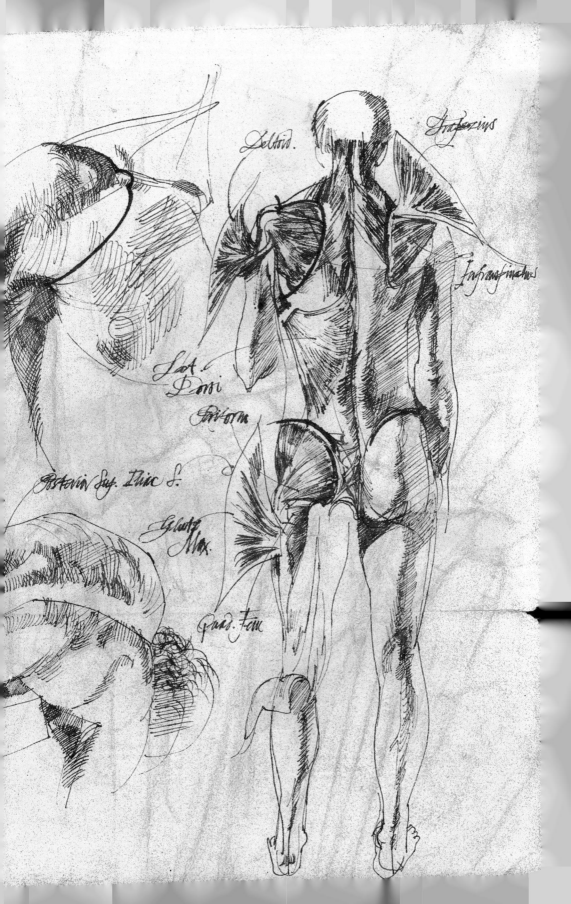

Deltoid.

Trapezius

Infraspinatus

Lat.
Dorsi

Piriform

Posterior Sup. Iliac S.

Glute
Max.

Quad. Fem

two cadavers a whole entity, there being aspects of each which are undesirable. Although in general the whole is responding adequately to the electrical fields, and the cellular tissue is showing indications of vital energy, the various parts are not knitting together, but are living as independent entities. The greater part of the anatomy refuses steadfastly to be associated with the superficial members, and the common sutures are already showing signs of atrohpy. Each section, for example the limbs, appears almost to be drawing into itself.

March 18th

The situation worsens. The painstaking surgery I undertook has come to naught, for the nerves, blood vessels and musculature have wasted and shrivelled away at the joining of sections. It occurs to me that perhaps I should reconsider the order of preparation. I had assumed that, before attempting to revitalise the brain, I should prepare the body that serves it. The calamity that is occurring could be the ignorant reaction of tissue which, undirected by an intelligence, retires into itself. Tomorrow I shall attempt to salvage the position by activating the cerebral cortex before deterioration is too far advanced. Igor shows an uncommon interest in the work and seems most reluctant to depart the laboratory at the end of the day. Despite my commands, I know that he visits it during the night. I will have to begin locking the chamber lest he interferes with any of the equipment. There are times when he scarcely seems to be of this earth. Apart from his fearful appearance, there is a dark aspect of his mind which I know nothing of. God alone knows what terrors he has known in his miserable life.

March 20th

I have attempted everything within my power to prevent the failure of the project. Although I am not satisfied that I have learned all I need of the cerebral function, I attempted to vitalise the brain in the hope of staying the disintegration of the corpse. At first I was encouraged in that a number of superficial responses, such as eye movement and the excitation of some facial muscles, were detectable, but as the experiment advanced, and the brain activity measurably increased, its distress became very marked. Finally, it seemed almost to generate its own electrical force, burned out the external connections and ceased to function at all. My desperate attempts to restore it were all fruitless and I fear that it is destroyed. I will open up the skull tomorrow in order to conduct an examination. Meanwhile, there seems little advantage in persisting with the stimulation of the rest of the anatomy, as there is no progress there to encourage me. All that lies upon that bench is meat alone, and poor meat at that.

Igor senses that all is not well, and lurks in the shadows out of my sight, as though afraid that I will blame him for the disaster. Poor fellow, I must seem almost like a god to his mindless perception.

March 21st

I was awake most of the night considering the failure of the experiment and debating its causes. I have now concluded that there is no singular fault in my intentions, but only in the way I chose to implement them. The body, for reasons I have not yet established, was in a state of great disorder. My attempts to vitalise the brain were, I am certain, fundamentally successful, but they introduced the intellect to a cacophony of stimuli from the disparate parts of the fragmented anatomy. No human mind could surely withstand the manifold agonies of a body so ill-composed. I suspect that the nervous centre of the brain could not accept life when every nerve advised it of physical calamity. I must try again, but this time I must awaken the central cons-ciousness before I even begin to bring to life its separate parts. This may allow the mind to adapt to the gradual introduction of its subservient members. Igor will have to journey again to Wurzburg.

March 27th

Once more the carriage has returned with its silent cargo, and this time Igor has surpassed himself. One of the bodies is particularly fine, he having managed to extricate it from the hospital within minutes of the owner's decease. I commenced work immediately, and have resolved to experiment upon the freshest corpse with the minimum of surgical interference. As soon as it was upon the table, I opened the braincase and implanted the electrical connections in the appropriate centres. Igor was able to conduct the infusion of plasma with little guidance from me, thus allowing me to proceed with greater speed. I have also immersed the body in a liquid solution to reduce the effects of gravity and minimise the degree of extraneous sensory stimulation. I remarked during the last abortive experiment that the animal tissue was adversely affected by gravity while subjected to the vitalising auras, and though living in essence, was uncertain of its fundamental form and allowed the gravitational influence to alter its shape to a degree.

March 30th

One of the arms is valueless, and the muscles have deteriorated, so it seems surgery is unavoidable. Much of today was therefore spent in replacing the imperfect limb. Although only the forearm was at fault, I decided to

overleaf
The tank in which Frankenstein stored the cadavers obtained by Igor. The one shown has already had its left arm removed.

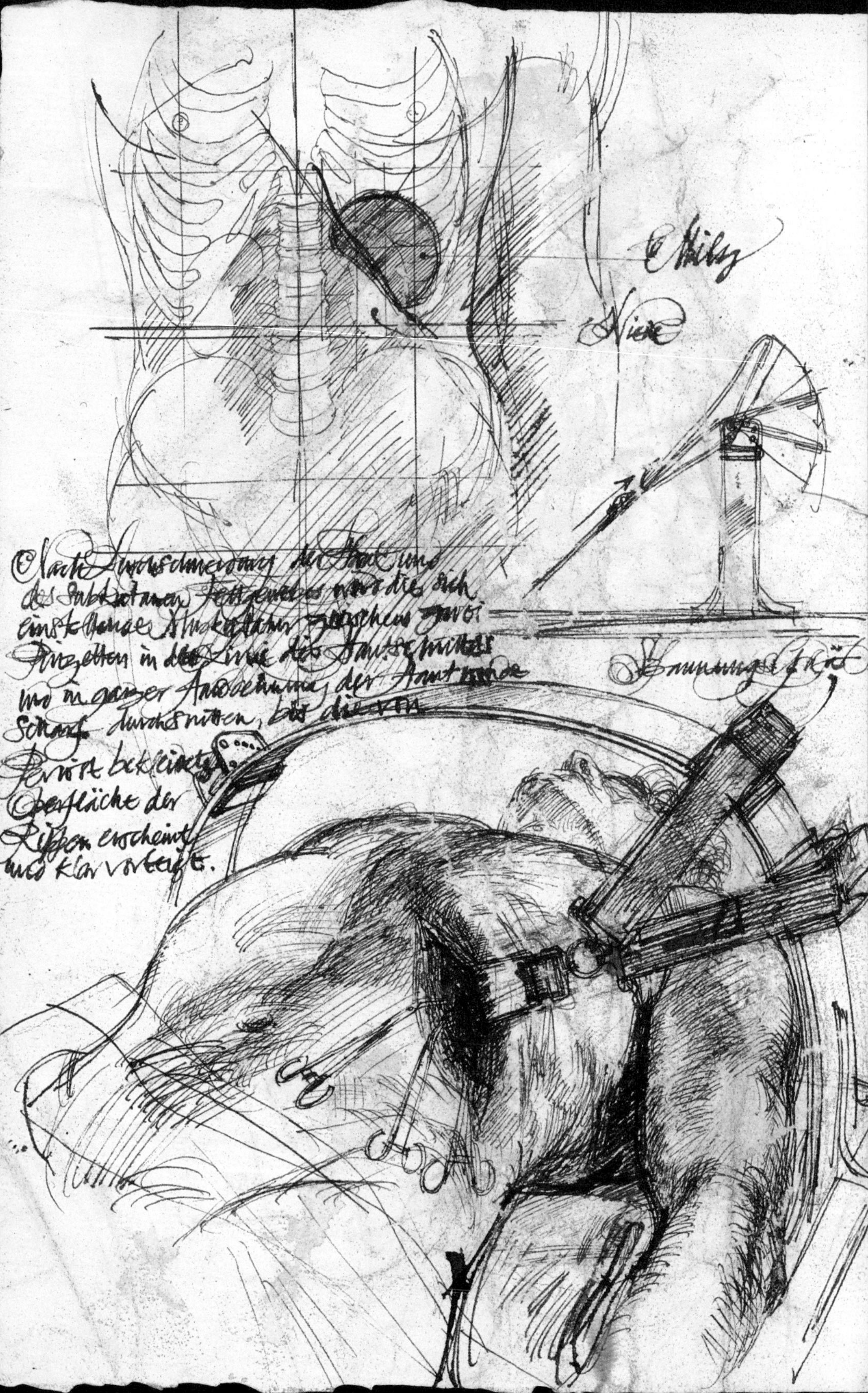

Milz

Niere

Nach Durchmessung der Haut und
des Subkutanen Fettgewebes wird die sich
einstellende Muskulatur zwischen zwei
Pinzetten in der Linie des Hautschnittes
und in ganzer Ausdehnung der Hautwunde
scharf durchschnitten, bis die VIII.

Spannungs...

Periost bekleidete
Oberfläche der
Rippen erscheint
und klar vorliegt.

replace the whole assembly as my work at Ingolstadt hospital convinced me that the larger the scale of transplantation, the more likely the body is to accept its new portion. I therefore exchanged the entire organ including the scapula, which required work on only the major muscle masses, blood vessels and so forth. While the exposed brain was being subjected to the various electrical auras, I investigated the internal structure. The corpse was that of a fairly young man and the organs were in fine condition apart from the spleen, which had been severely damaged and was probably the cause of death. I worked far into the night to remove the crushed remnants and replace them with the organ from one of the other cadavers. Before retiring I subjected it to a variety of stimulations, as it seems necessary to destroy the sense of self which is inherent in all human tissue. Unless this is achieved, the main part of the anatomy will always view a transplantation as a stranger to itself, and will refuse to incorporate it. That done I retired to my chamber without dining and went instantly to sleep.

March 31st

I awoke before the sun had arisen, dressed hurriedly and went directly to the laboratory. To my surprise Igor was already there, skulking by the door. I sent him to prepare some breakfast and set to work on the procedure for vitalising the brain. It is slow and laborious work as each area of the organ reacts to differing stimuli, and despite the fact that I have only succeeded in isolating and identifying those cerebral localities responsible for the main reflexes, the work consumed the greater part of the day. By nightfall, however, everything was in readiness and I began to feed electrical force into the network of resistors and exciters that determine the nature of the specific fields. The process of tissue stimulation is also lengthy, and after checking that all was in order, I retired to bed early in preparation for the real work that will commence tomorrow when the flow of current is amplified to vitalise the cell structures.

Later that night
I fell instantly into a deep slumber as soon as I lay upon my bed. I suppose I had slept thus for some hours when I was jarred into utter wakefulness by a shrieking of such a terrifying nature that I felt the blood stand still in my veins. I could not find the strength to raise my trembling limbs from the mattress. The screaming continued without ceasing and at last I forced my feet on to the floor. As I stood up the realisation struck me; no normal throat could produce such a dire sound, but the crushed and distorted larynx of a man who had been hung would not make a familiar noise. As I threw my gown about me I

opposite
Frankenstein was forced to develop items of equipment to assist him in surgical work that would normally have required more than one surgeon. Shown here is his design for a device to retract the rib cage for an operation to replace a damaged spleen.

deliberated on what agony could have wrenched a wail of terror from a dumb man. There could only be one explanation; the infernal fascination that the laboratory had exerted on that wretched creature must have enticed him into the chamber. The power produced by the converters is deadly, and fearing for Igor's life and the safety of my work, I hurled myself down the stairs without even pausing to take up a lamp. It was only my familiarity with the building that allowed me to plunge through the darkness, my mind torn between fury at the ignorance which placed all my work in jeopardy, and fear for Igor's life. Suddenly, as I ran headlong down the last corridor towards the fearful noise, something lying on the floor sent me sprawling. I fumbled in the pocket of my gown and struck a light from my tinder-box. There, in its feeble glimmer, stared the terror-twisted but silent face of Igor. I gazed transfixed at him, then slowly turned my head towards the laboratory door. What in God's name was in there? I climbed to my feet and, collecting a lamp, walked towards the door as the terrible scream pierced my brain. Fighting the fear that burned my throat, I stepped into the chamber and held up the lamp. Nothing stirred, but the sound emanated from the operating table where the carcass lay. I stared down at the dead face that lay amongst the cobweb of wires. The eyes were wide open, fixed in a horrible, unfocussed stare, and the mouth gaped wide. From it issued that unholy scream! Unable to think while the walls echoed so violently, I pressed a cloth into the throat, and paced about the room as I wracked my mind for an explanation of this terrifying phenomenon. I checked the current flows, but there was no malfunction that could have caused even a living creature such apparent distress. The cause could only lie within the waking brain encased in the mass of inanimate tissue.

As I stood there I sensed that once again the experiment was a failure, and that there was something I had overlooked. I deliberated deeply, my thoughts constantly distracted by the monotonous moan that continued unabated from the cadaver, until I was forced to recognise that once again I had failed. A feeling of despair descended on me as I slowly disconnected the various devices. Halfway through the task, the room fell silent and the eyes of the pale visage closed. I returned to bed feeling tired and utterly dispirited. Igor lay down outside my door.

April 1st

Igor was still outside when I stepped from my room this morning, and has not left me all day except when I entered the laboratory to inspect the body. He refused to enter and ran away when I attempted to coerce him into assisting me. Heaven knows what he imagined was taking place last night. I spent the day wandering in the forest trying to ascertain what had been the cause of the tragedy, and have come to the conclusion that even a dead brain retains a physical or chemical impression of identity. Somehow the young man who had perished in the Wurzburg hospital had been revived in the stimulated tissue. Though I find it hard to conceive, I must have inadvertently resurrected the soul of a dead man! That dreadful sound persists in my mind and I am unsettled by the thought of the agonies that his soul, or whatever entity it may have been, must have suffered at being brought back from the dark realm of Death to such circumstances. It is as though it were indeed the voice of Hell. God forgive me for that. I dare not risk a repetition and must consider carefully how I shall now proceed, for proceed I must.

April 2nd

I am resolved in what I must do, though that resolution has been bought at the cost of the greatest agonies of conscience. As in the case of organs or tissue that possess an intrinsic identity of self, and will scarcely tolerate the incorporation of tissue that is not of itself, so it must be with the brain. But whereas that essential identity can be overcome through the scientific application of electrical auras, the conscious identity of a mind that has lived and laid up the great store of memories and impressions that life provides cannot so easily be erased. I have considered the use of hypnotism as practised by Mesmer, but alas, I fear there will not be sufficient time for me to apply such methods before the awakened mind destroys itself with the horror of its alien fastness. The only solution can be the incorporation of the brain of a young child, upon which the lines of self consciousness have been but lightly etched. Such an organ, innocent of life and its place in the order of Nature, would surely suffer no more than a momentary confusion before it was able to accept its new vessel and the disappearance of the old.

April 5th

I passed these last days in the preparation of the laboratory and in making improvements to the mechanisms. This time I must not fail, for I have not the courage to overcome further failures. I now have the means to defeat that noisome adversary, Death, and lack only the clay from which to create the Immortal Knight who will lead mankind into the dawn of immortality.

overleaf
Pre-operative sketches for the replacement of an arm. Frankenstein considered that surgery was simplified, and the problems of rejection reduced, by the transplantation of whole limbs rather than parts of them.

1. Hautschnitt
2. Muskeldurchschneidung
3. Knochendurchsägung
4. Blutstillung
5. Nervenkürzung
6. Nahtvereinigung

Art. brachial
Vena brachial
Clavicula
Deltoid.
Biceps
Humerus
Pectoralis Major

I am resolved that my champion shall not present himself to the world as any less than a superman, a hero as of long ago. For if I am able to create a living being, then why should he not be a god-like creature? I shall set myself to build a living sculpture that will be in itself the representation of physical perfection. Until now I was content to simply return to life the imperfect bodies of frail mortals who had already succumbed to the scythe of the Reaper. With the skills I have now gained, I can construct an entirely new being as a magnificent temple for an innocent mind.

April 8th

Igor has returned and, through the offering of a princely donation to the hospital, has procured for me an excellent cargo. I will commence at once on the prodigious task of sculpting the physique of a god. Whilst I am engaged on this lengthy task, Igor will spend his days searching for the opportunity to acquire the appropriate brain, for this will be the single most important thing to accomplish.

April 12th

I have constructed, with Igor's assistance, a great operating table, upon which lie the bodies from whose anatomy I am constructing my paragon. My facilities are hard pressed to meet a demand far in excess of that which I had anticipated, but all seems to be well, and the cadavers remain in excellent condition. The torso of my creation is almost complete, and the various organs appear, according to my tests, to be functioning adequately. This afternoon I examined the heart, which is robust and responded strongly to the stimulation of that area of distinctive tissue in the muscle of the Atrium which governs the contraction of both the Atrium and the Ventricles. An unforeseen difficulty presented by an operation of such ambition is that of working among the scores of electrical filaments required, and I shall have to devise some solution before commencing the trans-plantation of the limbs, or else a disaster may occur. I have also devised a tent-like canopy which reaches to the floor and surrounds the tables, and within which I allow a carbolic solution to be introduced in a fine spray at intervals. My earlier experiments have indicated that this technique assists in preventing the onset of infection. The Wurzburg hospital authorities have replied to my letter but are adamant that they do not permit juvenile dissection and are therefore unable to furnish me with a suitable subject. This is a setback, damn their ignorance, but I have asked Igor to seek some alternative such as the

opposite
A sketch of the Sympathetic Nervous System which Viktor made prior to the implantation of electrodes in one of his subjects.

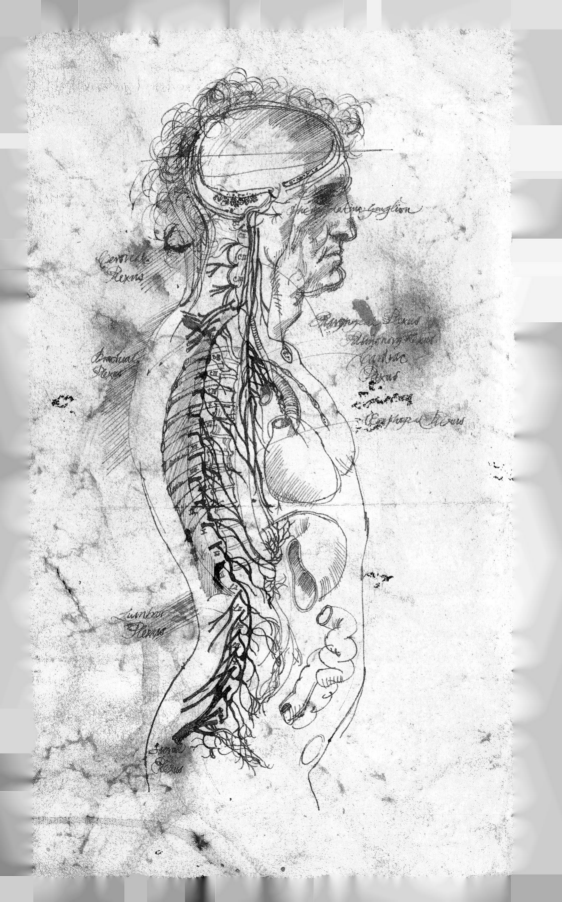

The Spheno-palatine Ganglion

Cervical Plexus

Brachial Plexus

Pharyngeal Plexus
Pulmonary Plexus
Cardiac Plexus

Esophageal Plexus

Lumbar Plexus

Sacral Plexus

TOURNIQUETS AND AMPUTATING INSTRUMENTS.

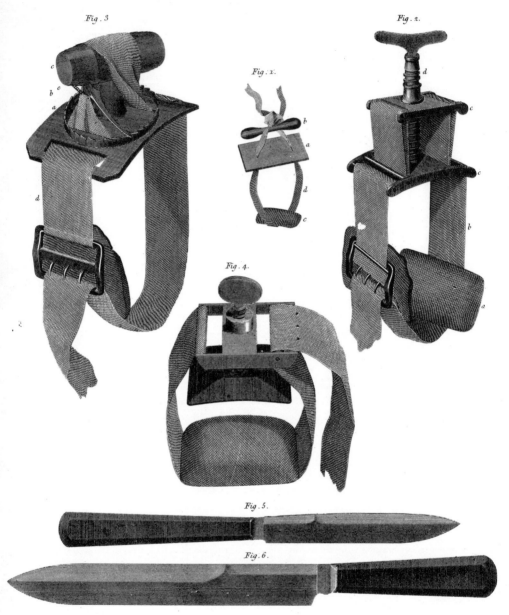

Fig. 3.

Fig. 1.

Fig. 2.

Fig. 4.

Fig. 5.

Fig. 6.

Published as the Act directs, June 1, 1808, by Longman & Rees, Paternoster Row.

Engraved by Wilson Lowry.

*Tourniquets and amputating
equipment of the kind that
would have been used by
Frankenstein at the university
and in his later work.*

procuring of the body of a newly deceased child from the town. There is still time to spare, but I fear lest this difficulty prove to be my undoing, for the auras will not sustain indefinitely the tissue of the part I have completed thus far.

April 14th

I have now completed the re-routing of all the severed vascular bundles where they exit from the torso, so that the circulatory system of the trunk is now self-contained. The heart is functioning correctly and my mechanical aerator is substituting for the lungs in a most satisfactory manner. The filamentation of both nerve and muscle tissue at the points where they are to be knitted into the extremities is almost complete, thank God, for this is a tiresome undertaking that fatigues me greatly. The strain of separating out the manifold fibres of each part is as great as that of splicing them together, and my eyes are most painful this night. Despite my exhaustion, I am not sleeping well, for there is so much to think of and one small item overlooked could be sufficient to undo all my careful labour. Tomorrow I shall begin surgery on the sacral region and hope to have one of the lower limbs attached and being fed by the vascular system.

April 15th

My head reels with the effects of such intense concentration, but at least the limb is now in place and circulation effected. I have tested the operation of the principal motor nerves and they are operating properly, but I must hope that the body itself will repair those minute cutaneous nerves that I have left unfastened. Some of these I can assist, with the application of current, to establish neural pathways for their re-generation, but others I must leave to the hand of fate. My strength is failing for lack of rest, but I must force myself to even greater speed, even greater care, as I am concerned that the magnetic generators on which all depends may prove unequal to the task of maintaining a constant production of power. One of them is already displaying some noticeable reduction in performance and I shall have to employ the only spare machine that I was able to construct before commencing work. Before re-tiring, I explained its construction to Igor, who tomorrow will attempt to recondition the faulty generator.

He has still not learned of any child in the town that is ill unto death, and I feel the first stirrings of alarm lest my great endeavour is frustrated at the last obstacle. There is, however, much work still to be done before I am ready to seat a mind within the skull.

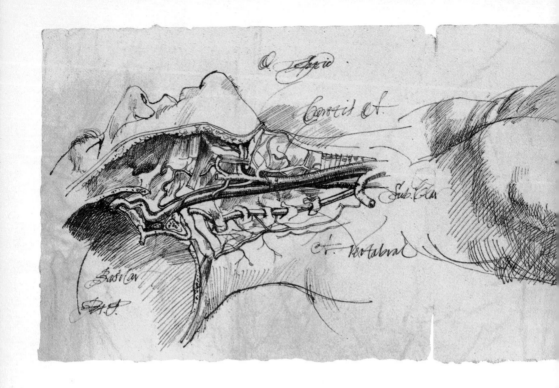

April 17th

Last night Satan sat upon my footstool and the dark corners of my room glimmered with the presence of his unholy acolytes. Whether I was sleeping or waking I know not, but this morning my limbs were heavy as though made of lead, and I feared lest their trembling should prevent me from continuing. I allowed myself a small draught of Laudanum, which improved my disposition greatly, and set to work once more. it was nightfall before I knew an hour had past, and the second leg is attached. As I had feared, Igor has succeeded only in almost completely destroying the imperfect generator that I set him to improve upon, and has burned himself with electricity into the bargain. I must now rely on those already at work, and trust to the Lord that they will not fail me. I could not bear to eat at all this night, and took Laudanum instead, that I might pass a restful night at last.

April 18th

My well-being is much improved today. I slept without waking until after sunrise, and indeed had to be woken by faithful Igor. I directed him once more to go to the town for provender and to pay attention to any rumour of

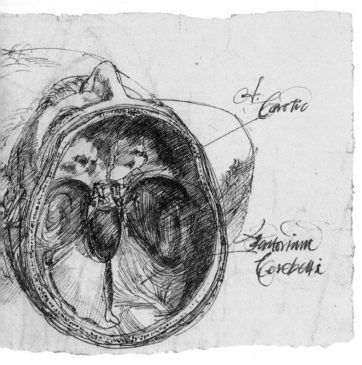

Studies made by Frankenstein in preparation for the introduction of the brain.

infantile sickness, as it will not be long before I am ready to complete the formation of the creature. I can risk no delay, and worked without ceasing on both the upper extremities, performing the operations in parallel as I have found it more efficient to duplicate each stage of surgery at one time. Though neither is yet complete, I believe they both shall be married to the frame tomorrow. I am in a cruel race against time; my own diminishing strength, the condition of the generators and the acquisition of a suitable brain being fearsome competitors. I dined alone this evening as even the presence of silent Igor distressed me, and prescribed myself another draught of Laudanum to keep at bay the fearful visions that lurk in my chamber.

April 19th

Had great difficulty in rising from my bed this morning, and felt much burdened by sleep until some hours after I had entered the laboratory. Nevertheless, the work on the upper extremities is well advanced and one is completed, appearing to react sufficiently well. There are problems attendant on the other as the Suprascapular nerve trunk is dry and wasted at the point where it passes through the Supra-spinatus muscle, and I fear that this portion has for some reason deteriorated beyond

The forester's cottage from which Frankenstein and Igor abducted the young child whose brain was used in Viktor's final creation.

recovery. I shall attempt to excise the affected section and introduce a similar segment from one of the other cadavers. It is yet another delay that I can ill afford. A further aggravation is that Igor, on entering the town, was set upon by ruffians and chased into the woods. He is disliked there, and apparently mistrusted, so that I am not confident that he will know of any mortality in sufficient time to inform me. I did not ever expect this quest to be an easy one, but I feel oppressed by the weight of circumstances conspiring against a successful outcome. The position is rapidly becoming serious, for I will not be able to maintain the condition of the carcass indefinitely, the auras being but a poor substitute for the forces generated by independent life. Desperate measures may be called for before many more days have passed, as I cannot allow the future immortality of Man to be threatened.

April 20th

Though I slept deeply last night, I do not feel refreshed, and can scarcely keep to my feet. I have brought a chair to the operating table and conduct much of the work seated.

I began to replace the portion of affected nerve fibre, but discovered that the deterioration was more extensive than I had thought, and it was necessary to substitute that branch which enters the Infra-spinatus muscle as well. That work completed to my satisfaction, I spent the rest of the day preparing the skull and spinal column for the last major surgical event. A brain must, absolutely must be obtained within three days, four at the very most, as there is already a minute but measurable diminution of the muscle tone of the lower extremities. I increased the output of the generators as much as I dared in order to stay the decline, but an improvement in the strength and quality of the auras is in a lesser proportion to the additional stress on the already suspect electrical apparatus.

I can no longer avoid a course of action which is utterly repugnant to me, but which I must undertake for the benefit of generations as yet unborn, the inheritors of an immortal destiny. I shall go clandestinely into the woods with Igor tomorrow, to where, so he tells me, a forester's dwelling lies. From there, God forgive me, we must seize and steal away the youngest child of that poor family. I have no choice, and can only console myself by considering that it will be easier for them to survive their loss than it would be for mankind to come to terms with a greater one. Another child can be conceived, but one such as mine may never otherwise be made. I shall resist the temptation to take Laudanum again this night as we must be gone from here before the sun rises. I shall finish writing and see that all is prepared for the morrow, then climb up to my room to wrestle with my dreams.

April 21st

There will be no sleep for me this night, as I lie washed by the seas of misery. Though my rational intellect consoles me, my heart is crushed beneath the weight of a guilty sorrow that such a dire course should be all that was open for me. I cherish the thought that God himself assisted us by arranging such circumstances as made the abduction swift and free from painful complication.

Igor and I had secreted ourselves in the dark undergrowth beside the glade where the rude dwelling stood, and watched the woodsman shoulder his axe and set off towards the town. Soon afterwards, the woman emerged with the youngest child and set off into the forest to gather kindling. We followed silently and watched as she cast about for faggots, straying further and further from the playing youngster. The moment came when she had passed from view, leaving her son engrossed in some infant preoccupation beneath the shadow of a great oak. One speedy manoeuvre, and the child was captured, then silenced with a distillation of alcohol and sulphuric acid

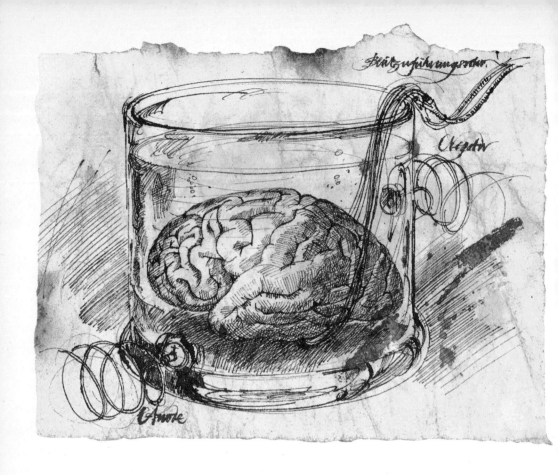

The brain of the woodman's child stored in an electrically charged container prior to its introduction into the prepared skull.

which I had prepared. It was but a small matter to transport the unconscious body back through the dank woods to the castle, though I was forced to muffle my ears against the distant and pitiful calls of the distraught mother wandering in search of her vanished offspring. Once returned, however, I could put aside my mortification in the activity of resuming my labours at the bench.

The poor child passed from sleep to death with the greatest ease I could allow, and never knew of its fate. Once its frame was but another carcass, I was more at ease and could undertake the crucial surgery with equanimity. By the time darkness had fallen, the living brain was encased in its new seat, washed in the vitalising ichor of the parent body. Tomorrow I shall activate the currents that will intensify the auras and awaken the latent forces that lie dormant within that giant frame. My jubilation as a scientist is abated by my misery as a man, and I am frightened to dwell on what I have done this day, but as I write, the soft balm of the Laudanum begins its work and I feel myself sinking gently into the soft mist of oblivion.

April 22nd

I awoke and went to the laboratory at first light, to find Igor already peering through the doorway at the great frame that lies within its cocoon of filaments. He scurried away at my approach, but returned at the sound of the generators as I increased the power efflux. The one small window was shuttered in case the light should distress the waking eyes, and the lamplight danced among the threads of metal as the chamber resonated with the hum of electrical force. I felt the perspiration streaming from my brow with the effort of concentration, for there were a thousand things to watch over and a hundred separate tasks to perform. The auras increased in strength until a bluish haze seemed to shimmer all about the still form of the creature. The tissue began to lose the transparency of inanimate flesh and small muscular tremors agitated the trunk and limbs. Suddenly the broad chest heaved convulsively once, then again. A pause, then the action was repeated and fell into a regular rhythm. It lived! Of their own volition, the lungs were drawing upon the air, and with trembling hands I removed the connections to the aerating machine. Without feeling for a pulse, I could hear the soft pounding of the heart increase, and with my breath still pent within my breast, I steadily reduced the power from the generators until they had stopped entirely. As they stood silent for the first time since my work began, the walls of the chamber echoed with the muffled, sonorous thudding of a newly born heart.

Dawning & Darkness

April 23rd

Only now, as I sit in the flickering shadows of my bedchamber, do I begin to sense the wonder of the great thing that has come to pass. The hand of God has led me through the lonely corridors of my days as the instrument of His Divine Purpose. I, mortal man, have twisted and turned in His grasp, unable to deny my own humanity, but always plucked back from life to continue in the quest that I believed was of my own making. I now understand that as John was the man of this world who prepared the way for the coming of the Messiah, so I am the herald of the next Adam. The Infinite Compassion that gave to us immortality in death has now bestowed upon us the promise of immortality in life, and the unhappiness of my passage through the world is a price of little consequence.

Throughout this day, I have felt myself drawn irresistibly to the side of the creature, and have gazed in humble admiration at the miracle that lay before me, its great breast drawing in and expelling the life-giving vapours, and echoing with the soft resounding of the mighty engine beneath its ribs. Now that the feat has been accomplished, my role is little more than that of a caretaker, tending and nurturing the body as its healing powers seek to repair the ravages of my knife and knit together the disparate portions of itself. I recreate the auras at intervals to assist the process of healing, but my main duty is now finished and the rest is for God Himself to accomplish. It will be some time before the creature is conscious; there is no place for intelligent awareness in the battle that rages throughout every fibre of its being. I am ill at ease when there is so little that I can do to influence the outcome, and can only console myself that God would not allow the work of a lifetime to be cast aside through His own neglect.

April 25th

Igor has started to overcome his fear of the laboratory and its silent guest at last, and will now enter to assist me in tending the patient. He is often to be found close by the table whereon the creature lies.

My confidence regarding its post-operative recovery is sorely tested, as the condition of the tissues is

deteriorating. Yesterday and today have been devoted to testing the operation of the internal organs, and though there are certainly many deficiencies, all is essentially in order. There is no more to do than maintain the sterility of the tent enclosing the table, and clean the wounds.

I must be more positive in my attitude and place my faith in God, for once recovery is made, there will be as much to do in preparing the creature for life and society as there has been in forming him. He will be a child in the body of an earthly god, the vanguard of a new race of Man, and must be educated in his inheritance with wisdom and care.

Thousands of fine copper electrodes formed a complex web over the body, passing through a wooden loom before connecting with the electrical apparatus.

May 3rd

At last there is progress. Though the extent of the creature's surgery would be beyond the abilities of others to repair, the maintaining of the auras and the hand of God have wrenched the mutilated carcass from the dark fist of Death, and its temperature, pulse and reflexes are more nearly usual. I have begun to reduce the periods of electrical stimulation to allow the body's resources to exercise themselves more fully, and Igor willingly maintains a careful watch during my absence. This

gratifying change has heartened me immeasurably and I am able significantly to reduce the amounts of sleeping draught to which I had become accustomed. I had not appreciated the extent to which I had come to depend on this dangerous substance.

May 6th

What a day for rejoicing is this! I was deep in contemplation after a wholesome meal when Igor cast himself into the room in a state of the greatest agitation, plucking at my sleeve and peering back through the doorway as though pursued by Satan himself. Unable to ascertain the cause of his consternation, but aware that its cause lay in the laboratory, I ran down the dim corridors and into the humming chamber. I went directly to the creature and inspected it minutely, but could find no cause for alarm therein. Igor scuttled to my side and held my sleeve, jabbing with his finger at the nearest hand of the body that lay silent before us. I could see nothing that could have excited him so, though I peered intently at the place. Suddenly, unbelievably, the pale, bony digits twitched, were still, then slowly and awkwardly stretched themselves, only to relax once more. I staggered in amazement, my heart seeming to fall still within my breast.

Köhre aus durchlässigem Membran

Fighting to steady my mind, I executed the accustomed pattern of activity; to measure the pulse, feel the brow and to note the rate of respiration. The familiarity of this procedure calmed me, and I approached the head in order to peer into the eyes as I had done so frequently in the past. As I extended my hand to raise the waxy lids, they flickered and I paused. Then they lifted abruptly and I stared into those yellowish orbs, now lambent with the uncanny glow of life. They cast about slowly until they came to rest on me, and as our glances met, a flood of strange emotion swept through my veins. Those twin doors opening into the darkness of a naked mind seemed to grow in size until I saw nothing else. It seemed as though they would engulf me and pull me through the gates of time into eternity that lay beyond. I was suddenly overwhelmed by a feeling of terror and loathing that paralysed me, and instead of the glory of the new Adam, I saw the spawn of hell, imprisoned in a lacerated, suppurating carcass. A small whimpering penetrated my frozen mind, forcing me to tear my eyes away from those of the creature, and I turned to where Igor hung upon my arm. The sight of his terrified eyes broke the sininster spell, and as the dark pall evaporated from my spirit, I turned again towards the face of the creature. Though still fixed upon me, its eyes had lost their unearthly quality and I saw instead the eyes of a child in desperate agony, which suddenly dulled and

The device shown here is similar to the modern kidney machine in its basic form, and was obviously designed to remove impurities in the blood of the subject.

closed as a great tremor ran through the huge frame. The last shreds of uncertainty fled as my fear for the safety of the creature increased, but my hurried examination revealed nothing of concern, and all the unconscious systems seemed to be functioning properly. There was no further occurrence of this kind, and after reassuring Igor and attending to the equipment, I returned to the solitude of my chamber to consider the fearful emotions that had so affected me at the time of the creature's brief awakening.

May 7th

The uneasiness of yesterday is quite dispelled and I am jubilant at the prospect of the creature's emergence from the coma in which it has lain for so long. Unless there is some unlikely relapse, the tide of vitality will flow ever more strongly through its organs until all the ravages of surgery have been erased. I long for the time when I shall be able to converse with it, and instruct it in the business of living. Once it has learned not only the mechanics of living, but also the skills of intellectual action, I shall introduce it to the world of men. No longer will mankind be forced to scurry out its span beneath the ungracious yoke of Death, no longer will great minds be pressed to dust before their greatest gifts have been presented to their fellow creatures. Those that will perish in the coming days will be returned to life, and those that are living will do so for all time. Then will the furthest realms of knowledge be explored and defined.

May 12th

Each day that has passed has seen the creature awaken for ever lengthening periods of time, and it has begun to make attempts at moving itself. The evil that I imagined was lurking behind its eyes that first day has made no further appearance.

I have now disconnected the electrical filaments, though they are in readiness should the creature show signs of regression, and the couch is now free from the filamentous web that had hindered the liberty of the creature. Igor devotes considerable time to observing the creature and is constantly trying to attract its attention by displaying various items before its eyes. I allow him to continue as it displays some slight interest and the activity will stimulate its mind. I am tempted to christen it Dionysus after the Greek god who was torn from limb to limb by the Titans and then restored to life by Rhea. It seems amxious to move about and I have decided to physically restrain its body with thongs as the healing is insufficiently advanced and there is risk of disturbing the

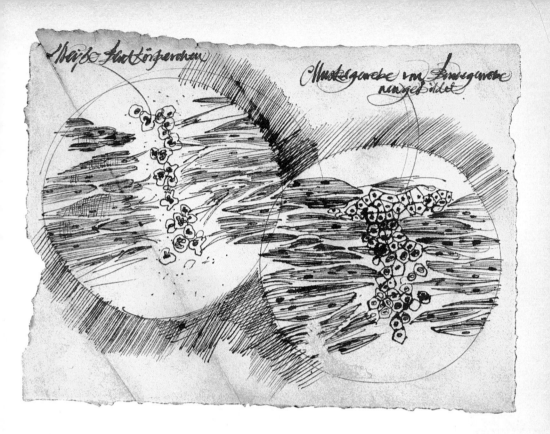

many sutures. Nevertheless the outlook is encouraging, and I hope to allow it to take restricted exercise quite soon.

A microscopic study showing Frankenstein's attempts to overcome the problem of tissue rejection. The first image illustrates the action of white corpuscles in the injured area during rejection, the second shows the formation of connective tissue after his treatment.

May 18th

Something is amiss and I am at a loss as to what phenomenon could be disturbing the creature. For the last two days I have found evidence that it casts about wildly in its sleep, for the areas of skin which lie beneath the thongs are much chafed and the tender flesh is torn in places. After the first occasion, I fed to it a small measure of sleeping draught that it might not be disturbed in its slumber, but it proved valueless as the skin was even more inflamed and broken. Though I maintained a close watch throughout the day I saw nothing untoward in its behaviour.

May 19th

I awoke unusually early and repaired to the laboratory without any particular purpose in mind. There I witnessed Igor taunting the creature unmercifully by

passing an uncovered lamp before its eyes. The creature was casting about in a desperate fashion. My fury knew no bounds as I observed how the restraints cut deep into the delicate flesh, and I regret that I struck violently at Igor, knocking him to the floor. He lay a moment, anger and anguish displaying themselves alternately in those dark eyes, then he sprang to his feet and fled into the corridor. I turned to the creature to reassure myself that no permanent injury had been inflicted and it looked at me piteously as though afraid that I too might mean it harm. My ministrations eventually had a calming effect and succeeded in persuading it to take some of the nutrient I had prepared. I then sought Igor to make amends for my hasty behaviour and to explain the reasons for my displeasure, but he was not be be found and appears to have left the castle entirely. I hope that he will return as he is of value to me and I have grown fond of his misshapen form and pathetic adoration of me.

May 21st

Igor stayed away for two nights and my search yesterday did not reveal his hiding place. He eventually returned some time this evening, as I found supper prepared. After I had eaten, he emerged from some dark corner to remove the dishes and I deemed it best not to refer to the incident at all. Meanwhile the creature has improved immeasurably and I have begun work on a device which will allow it to move in a limited fashion. I will continue to restrain it during the night.

May 23rd

I am once again sleeping poorly. I think that these inactive days are too great a contrast to my years of intense labour. Nevertheless there are so many smaller matters to attend to; the life I have engendered must now be nurtured and instructed. Although I have always anticipated that my efforts would be somewhat crude in comparison with those of Nature herself, I had hoped that She would compensate for my deficiencies, and be generous enough to build upon the foundations that I have laid. But it seems that She is a trifle reluctant to do so. For some time now I have laboured to encourage the joining in harmony of the disparate portions of the creature's anatomy, but it is clearly distressed and suffers growing discomfort. Of particular concern are the abdominal sutures, which weep copiously and exude a purulent discharge which threatens to undo my work. Despite my care there is an infection which inflames the adjoining flesh, and the attendant irritation encourages the beast to disturb the dressings. I fear that I shall have

opposite
Viktor's studies of the visible effects of tissue rejection following major surgical reconstruction. His work was also dogged by the problem of sepsis.

overleaf
The diary records that Frankenstein was forced to devise a frame to assist the creature to stand and walk. Shown here are his preparatory sketches.

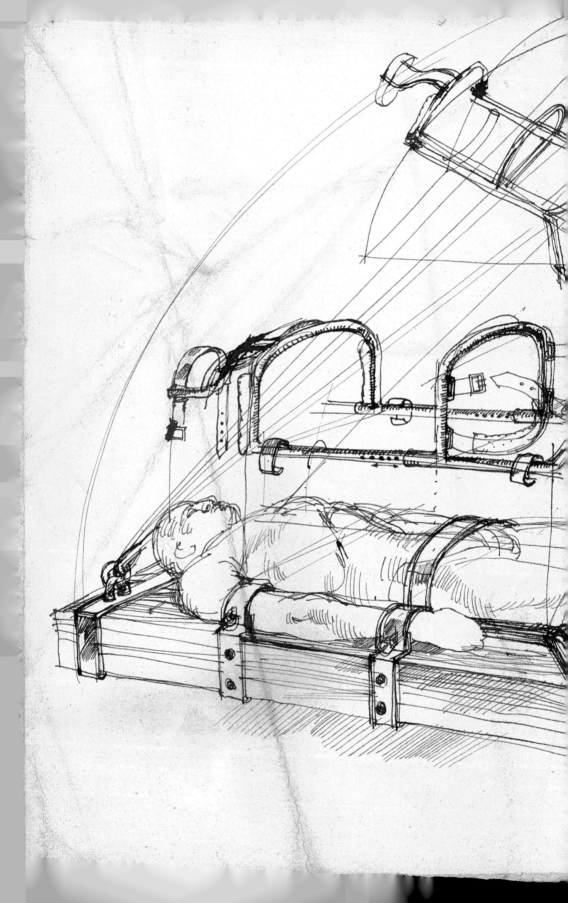

to continue to employ the restraints through the day as well as at night, but am loth to employ the services of Igor. There continues to be a sinister quality to his interest in the creature; he is at once fearful of its strength, yet feels a scornful repugnance for its ignorance and unnatural aspect. Though I may flatter myself unduly, I suspect that he is also jealous of my interest in and attentiveness towards the creature. He stares for hours through the small window in the door of the laboratory, but scurries away in a most furtive fashion when I approach. He is now forbidden to enter the room unless upon my express instructions, but I am certain that he disobeys.

May 24th

At last there seems to be some progress in the development of the creature's senses. On repeating the usual tests this day, I detected a small movement of the iris in response to light directed into the right eye, and the improvement was more marked when the experiment was repeated a few hours later. The left, however, is less encouraging. There is a distinct cloudiness within one of the vestibules of the eye, or a deterioration of the lens itself, and I fear that its power of vision is in jeopardy. I shall consider drawing off some of the aqueous humour for examination.

It will soon be night once more, and I fear it. So many malevolent visions lurk like footpads in the corners of my mind. There is a cusp between waking and sleeping which belongs to Satan, and the portal thereof opens into the loathesome vaults of Hell itself. I fear lest such a gate lies also in the mind of the creature I have made. I remember still the shadows that dwelt deep within those orbs that first day, and I am terrified lest in its ignorance it lifts the latch to admit the rabid darkness, and makes itself the plaything of evil.

May 26th

I awoke from my fitful slumbers at a fearful shrieking from beneath my chamber. My flesh crawled in horror at the thought that a repetition of the earlier calamity might have occurred, and made my way with cautious haste to the laboratory. There, to my amazement, I beheld the creature crouching beneath the couch on which it had been secured. The stout thongs which had secured its limbs were burst asunder, though how this had been accomplished I knew not. It was in the direst pain and plucked convulsively at the bruised flesh, which had parted at the effort. I managed to force a sleeping draught between its teeth before summoning Igor to assist me in moving the huge bulk back onto the couch. He did not come, and as I strained to lift the unresponsive weight I noticed a tattered fragment of cloth entwined in its fingers which could only have come from Igor's coat. I am suddenly afraid that the latter's unholy fascination will have some dire consequence.

I passed the rest of the night on a rude bed outside the door of the laboratory but slept not. Tomorrow I shall attempt to cauterise the sutures to kill this wretched infection, but am fearful of the unexpected and prodigious strength of the creature. A small insistent voice deep within me whispers horrid doubts that disturb me alarmingly. Can this great thing that I have done be a preposterous jest perpetrated by some evil agency? But no, it cannot be. There is no blemish on my intentions, and God could not permit any dire calamity to arise from my selfless and benevolent dedication.

May 29th

I am both encouraged and alarmed at the extraordinary pace at which the creature improves. The infection has almost departed and its strength increases daily. With a little help it can now stand, and has begun to shuffle ponderously about in the exercise frame I have contrived. It has not yet displayed any desire to venture beyond the confines of the laboratory, finding sufficient to occupy its attention in the objects I bring. I have no further contact with Igor, though I have seen him lurking at a distance from me. Whatever bond existed between us is now destroyed and I believe that I shall have to evict him from the castle. Thank God that I have little need of him now.

June 6th

A most dreadful thing has come to pass. Last night I was again woken from a tormented dream, not by a scream as before, but by some vague presentiment. The feeling persisted, preventing further rest, so I dressed and descended to the laboratory in order to reassure myself as to the creature's well being. I pressed against the door to open it but it resisted my effort, and it was with the greatest difficulty that I forced it ajar. A weight obstructed its movement, and as soon as the aperture was large enough to admit me, I held the lamp before me and pulled myself through. At my appearance, or rather that of the lamp, there was a scuffling and whimpering sound, and as I lifted the light to peer into the room I saw the creature crawl into a shallow recess. I shielded the flame which was the source of its distress and as I did so remembered the obstruction that had hindered my entry. I glanced down at the floor, then staggered back at the monstrous

sight that met my eyes, for there lay the contorted and bloodspattered carcass of Igor, his limbs almost rent from his body and his dark face crushed as though by some fearsome blow. Broken teeth protruded from the mangled welter of torn skin and gore, and a single blood-speckled eye stared wildly from the ruin. A great weight seemed to press upon me and my legs could scarce support me as I leaned against the chill wall. O God that it should come to this!

June 7th

All night I walked through the empty, decaying corridors or stood upon the windswept walls, the emptiness within me seeming to echo with the mournful crying of the air as it moved among the crumbling buttresses and quoins of this dismal place. I scarcely noticed the rising sun as it climbed through the dank mist that coiled among the mossy trees below, until its warmth drew out the chill from my face, and with it the desolation that leeched me from within. I began to recover my composure as the growing light drove out the last wisps of that terrible night, and recognised that Igor's first unhealthy absorption could only have led to this miserable conclusion. Now that the play was acted out to the last dismal scene, my task was to continue with my work unhindered. Once more I am alone in my quest and must continue as I have always done. So resolved, I returned to the laboratory and found the beast asleep upon its couch. Apart from a burn upon its neck and jowl, caused no doubt by the lamp that lay smashed beside the couch, there was no damage of consequence. Perspiring with the effort, I dragged Igor's broken body from the room and down the stairs to a corner of the old courtyard where I interred it. When the creature eventually awoke I devoted most of the day to regaining its confidence and reassuring it as to my intentions. I do not believe that it understands what it has done, and hope, therefore, that the growth of its intelligence will not be impeded. I go now to my bed in the hope that sleep will repair the ravages of these events.

June 14th

Igor's swarthy face is just one among the many more frightful phantasms flitting between the shafts of moonlight that pierce the Stygian gloom around the blessed island of my bed. I am resigned to greater terrors yet to come, and know that Death has sent the legions of Madness to turn me from conquest. I shall not yield to their ghastly clamour, for God will send his angels in the final onslaught against the citadel of Mortality, and together we shall drive the Fiend from the battlements. The

opposite
These drawings of Igor, Frankenstein's curious assistant, are the only ones known to exist, and were probably made soon after his arrival at Schwarzstein castle. Frankenstein was obviously interested in the deformities caused by Igor's narrow escape from death on the gallows.

creature seems also to have obliterated its tormentor from its memory, yet I am certain that the unhappy episode has strengthened the unspoken bond between us. Though it cannot yet speak words, it utters emphatic sounds and gives signs of pleasure at my appearance in the laboratory. Though the effort affords it considerable discomfort, it applies itself diligently to exercising in the frame, and each day I increase the amount of time that it devotes to this simple recreation. The muscles of its limbs are benefiting visibly.

Once each week I sedate it and implant the termini for several hours to allow the auras to reinforce the muscle growth and to remove the effects of strain which are occasionally incurred. But it is as essential that its mind be similarly instructed, and I have begun the delicate task of teaching it simple skills. It learned, with commendable speed, to identify the odd one among a collection of similar objects, and can separate various fruits into their correct categories with little difficulty.

Despite the physical progress of the creature, I am still concerned about the slow improvement in its nervous co-ordination. My greatest worry following the extensive operations performed on the creature was regarding the success of the regeneration of its nerve fibre. I employed the method of using electrical current, passed between two adjacent portions of severed nerve, to create a dynamic pathway along which the nervous tract would regenerate. This treatment, with which I had experimented at Ingolstadt, has proved outwardly successful, but there is nevertheless a marked discrepancy between the creature's intended movement and the effective result. The most common symptom is over-reaction when a movement is effected with greater speed or strength than the task requires. For this reason it continues to fail at attempts to feed itself, most of the food being spread about the floor or spilt upon its breast. It is noticeable that when it is absorbed in attempting to perform a specific task, other parts of its anatomy cease to be under its control. I have little natural patience with this work and find it wearisome in the extreme, so I must take care not to yield to my impetuosity. It is only my dislike of retiring to that wretched chamber above that prevents me from shirking my duty in this matter.

June 25th

At last the progress of the creature is more clearly marked. Physical co-ordination is much improved and it will soon be able to forgo the exercise frame entirely, although I shall have to equip it with some means of assisting the lower limbs in supporting its weighty torso. Though feeding continues to be a messy affair, most of the nourishment reaches its proper destination, but more significant is the sense of self-government that stirs within its breast. When listening secretly outside the door, I have on a number of occasions detected movement within, whereas previously it would not stir from its litter unless at my insistence. This is most heartening and inspires me in these otherwise tedious lessons. As I watch it bent in childlike concentration over the puzzles I set before it, I feel a curious blend of emotions. One instant I am filled with a paternal tenderness inspired by its utter innocence, another finds my heart stilled in awe of this thing that I have made, this triumph beyond the world's imaginings. All my bitter days have been transmuted from base metal to a virtue more potent than gold in this glorious alchemy, and the light of eternal vitality that waits to burn in the torch of science throughout the world blazes in the face of the hollow-eyed predator who has ravaged Man through all the ages.

I must beware; the battle is far from won and Hell itself is ranked against me, pressing close upon me in the grim wastes of the night.

July 5th

Last night was the worst that I have yet experienced. I could not allow myself to sleep until the sky had begun to lighten, for the terrible armies hurled themselves upon me throughout the hours of darkness and the noisome stench of Hell filled my nostrils till I could scarcely draw breath. God be with me, for I cannot withstand such fury for long, my mortality betrays me and my mind grows daily weaker. So fiercely did I resist their foul onslaught that I awoke with my palms torn by my own clenched fingers.

It was with difficulty that I raised myself from my bed, dressed and ventured forth to the laboratory. The creature was already beside the door when I entered, and indicated its pleasure at my arrival by swaying softly from side to side as it stood encased in the exercise frame, emitting the peculiar, throaty rumblings that pass for communication. Anxious to throw off the lingering sensations of that horrid night, I threw myself into the day's duties with a vigour I thought I had lost. My energy seems to have inspired the creature, as we made much progress in the lessons. Co-ordination has improved enough to allow the use of drawing instruments, which it employs with ponderous concentration in duplicating the examples I set before it. My persistence in continuing to present it with tasks requiring no mean delicacy of touch and control has been rewarded by its growing ability to feed itself in a pleasing manner. Whether as a result of my relief at having survived the night unscathed, or the satisfaction of recording significant progress in the creature's demeanour, I felt positively light-headed

overleaf, left
These working diagrams on nerve regeneration in living tissue are remarkable in anticipating modern techniques. The passing of electrical current between sections of severed nerve to establish a pathway for new growth has only been developed in recent years.

overleaf, right
For some time after the animation of the creature, the lower limbs proved unable to support its full weight. It progressed from a walking cradle to these leg braces, devised by Frankenstein.

Cutaneus Brancii Lateralis

Animus

Median

brach
intus

Ulnar
Med. antebrach.

Animus

Dura Mater

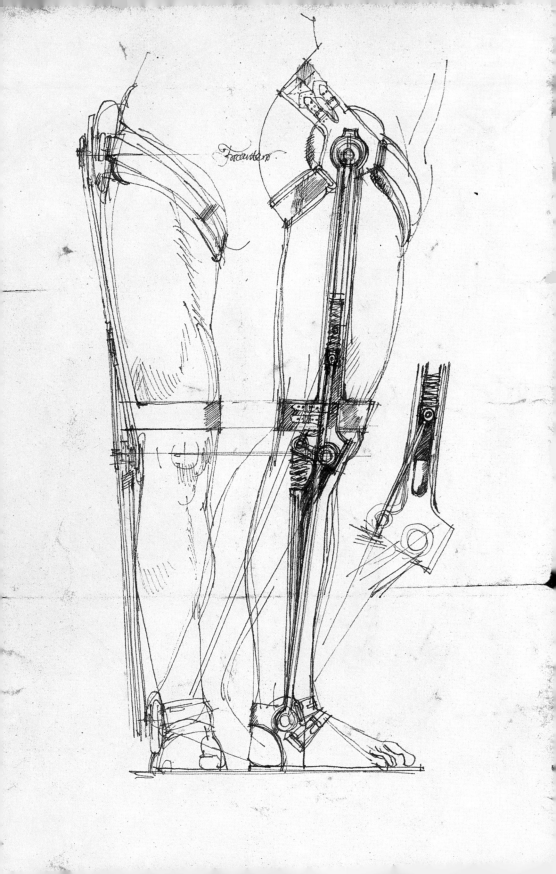

throughout the day and even had occasion to chuckle at the thought of the beast becoming skilled enough in social graces to take its place at any well-mannered table. As the sound escaped my lips, I was abruptly reminded of the time that has passed since last I had cause for amusement, and indeed the unaccustomed noise startled the creature enough to cause it to move nervously away from me. How I long for the day when my solitude can be put aside and I can lead my Adam forth into the world of men as proof of the salvation that awaits them through the application of scientific thought. The sense of well-being that has flourished in me today is fast evaporating as the sky darkens and I must once more enter the demon lists.

July 29th

I am at my lowest ebb for many months, lower even than at the time of poor Igor's death. I feel my ability to stand firm against the demonic hordes weakening, and they have begun to sally forth even during the hours of daylight. I am distraught at their indefatigable determination and begin to fear for our safety. I know this threat to be real and can no longer pretend that they are of my own imaginings, for as they have gained in strength, so has the momentum of the creature's recent progress begun to deteriorate. It is restless and inattentive, no longer taking delight in the tasks I exhort it to undertake. Its feeding is also most irregular; at times it refuses to take nourishment at all, yet later will consume all that I place before it and still appeal for more. I am unable to discover any symptoms that would indicate a physical disorder; indeed it is in better health than ever before. It has no further use for the exercise frame, and paces about the laboratory ceaselessly, until the sound of the metal leg supports grates upon my ear unbearably. Though I pray unceasingly, I am failing in hope, for God seems to have deserted me. And yet I cannot believe that he would forsake me now, when our common victory is so close at hand.

August 9th

Satan works within me now, by attempting to stir up a fear of the creature I have made with my own hands. For fleeting moments I see it as an ugly and dangerous thing, which I know it is not, and I have to impress upon myself that its apparent antagonism is but an invention of the Devil. Nevertheless my attempts at educating the creature have failed entirely for the present and it will not eat with me, but withdraws to a corner in order to devour the meat which it snatches from the table. At night I hear

opposite
An extraordinary record of Frankenstein's attempts to educate the creature. On the left are the models drawn by Viktor and on the right are the monster's attempts to reproduce them.

Ein Scheußliches Verbrechen

In den frühen Stunden von Gestern wurde in einem Vorort der Stadt der furchtbar zerfleischte Körper eines Fräuleins Frieden aufgefunden. Herr Bilsden, der Förster in dieser Gegend, stieß auf den zergliederten Torso in einem entlegenen Dickicht in der Nähe seiner Hütte, nachdem er dorthin gegangen war, um eine Reihe von seltsamen Lauten im Unterholz zu ergründen.

Das Verbrechen war nur wenige Augenblicke vor seiner Ankunft begangen worden, und der Förster will den Angreifer, während dieser weglief, flüchtig zu sehen bekommen haben. Nach seiner Entlassung aus dem Gerichtshof, wo er von den Behörden verhört worden war, behauptete Herr Bilsden, es sei, "ein Ungeheuer gewesen, von enormem Wuchs und schlecht gekleidet." Dazu habe der Mörder mit einer unirdischen hohen Stimme aufgeschrien, wie ein kleines verwundetes Tier, als er in den dunklen Wald verschwand.

Dieses, es sei hier berichtet, ist das zweite solcher unmenschlichen Verbrechen in zwei Wochen innerhalb der Stadtgrenzen. Die empörten Bürger verlangen jetzt Versicherungen vom Bürgermeister des Ortes, daß ausreichende Maßnahmen getroffen werden, um das Ungeheuer gefangenzunehmen. Ein Sprecher hat eben heute bestätigt, daß einige Vertreter aus den Reihen der Bürger ernes ... wurden die

den städtischen Instanzen beistehen sollen. Ferner behauptete er, derselbe Schuldige trage die Verantwortung für diese beiden scheusslichen Verbrechen, da beide Opfer Angriffen von derselben furchtbaren Grausamkeit unterworfen wurden. Sicherlich hätte die körperliche Kraft des wutenden Angreifers, von der die Art der Wunden ausreichenden Beweis lieferte, nur bei einem Individuum vorkommen könne ...

Man durchforscht jetzt sorg fältig die ganze C ... festzustellen v ... aufhä...

A contemporary newspaper account of a brutal murder which took place near the castle. The nature and extent of the victim's mutilation convinced local people that some unnatural agency was responsible, but as there were no witnesses to the crime, the illustration must be considered speculative.

it casting about the chamber in an impetuous fashion and have taken to sleeping outside the locked door in case it injures itself. Thank God my own nocturnal struggles have diminished somewhat and I am able to rest for greater periods.

August 14th

The monster prowls the dim corridors incessantly, its piteous, fluting cries echoing among the darkened rooms to which it is restricted. I am deeply disturbed by the constant attempts it makes to escape, but dare not allow it to move freely in the castle. A sense of desperate solitude fills me with painful recollections of past times, and though imprisonment may be irksome to the creature, how much worse it is for me whose incarceration is of my own making.

August 21st

Would to God that I had set an aperture in the door to the creature's apartments. It has ceased to make those cries which I had found both moving and alarming, and now contents itself with infrequent grunts and murmurings. If I press my ear to the door, I can sometimes hear it shuffling and moving beyond, but if I attempt to open the door enough to peer into the dim chamber, it hurtles from the gloom towards me with such venom and rage that I fear for my life. It will not even permit me to place food inside the hall, and I have had to construct a device to lower food to the window below a balcony in order to prevent the beast from starving. The battle is between God and Satan now, for my strength is spent and events have swept beyond me. Curiously, it is as though the madness has ridden over me, its eyes on a greater foe ahead, for I am hardly troubled in my sleep these nights.

August 23rd

I was startled this morning by the arrival of a delegation from the village. It is the first time any soul from there has called upon me, but it was no social visit. They came to enquire of me as to whether I might have knowledge of the whereabouts of two lovers that had last been seen in the forests nearby. The manner of their asking suggested that they thought me to be responsible for their disappearance. Idiots; my solitude is all the more bearable when I consider the alternative of their prolonged company.

August 25th

I noticed an unpleasant scent of suppuration as I passed the door to the creature's chambers, and I fear it may not be consuming all the meat that I deliver on the hoist. I am concerned lest it consume some of the fallen scraps which have festered, and may sicken. But I know not how I may safely gain entrance to enquire. I must cut an aperture in the door and devise a means of enticing the beast to swallow a sleeping draught. This will be difficult to accomplish as there is ample water available within the rooms it occupies.

August 27th

My work on the door was interrupted by another
visitation from the magistrate and his henchman.
Another villager has vanished under mysterious
circumstances and they seem even more convinced that I
am the culprit. They wished to enter to satisfy
themselves that the wretched oaf was not secreted here
against his will, but this I could not permit. After a heated
discussion they reluctantly withdrew and, closing the
gates on them, I returned to my labours. When at last the
task was completed, I peered into the darkness beyond,
but was unable to survey more than a portion of the
apartment. The air inside was heavy with the stench of
decay, to a degreee which caused me to gag and recoil.
Tomorrow I must enter at whatever the cost or danger
and subdue the creature, for its very existence may be at
risk. How I shall move its great bulk to the laboratory
without assistance I know not, but that I shall have to
consider once the greater problem of its subjugation has
been solved.

August 28th

The night seemed endless and full of suffering. I had
allowed myself to fall into complacency, and was not
prepared for the reappearance of that ghastly spectral
host. Monstrous visions taunted me from the darkness.
My father seemed to call to me from the black shroud that
emcompassed my bed, and I glimpsed him cavorting
among all manner of foul wraiths. The thick, sweet reek
of suppuration pervaded the room as though rising from
the depths of Hell itself, and even the pale morning
sunlight was unable to dispel the strangling odour. I
must enter the creature's den today, and have fashioned a
crude trolley on which I shall attempt to move the beast
should I succeed, as indeed I must, in subduing it.

August 29th

O dear God, what unholy horror have I visited upon the
world! My very soul shrieks with utter despair and I feel
the dank mists of madness seeping and gathering in the
corners of my tormented mind. I had expected today's
adventure to de distasteful, but dear Lord, not such a
nightmare as this. I had pulled the litter to the creature's
door and prepared a phial of the alcohol and sulphuric
acid distillate with which I intended to render the beast
unconscious. But there was no sign of it through the
aperture, and though I called and hammered on the
wood, I could not summon it. I became convinced that
my worst fears had been realised, that it had already

partaken of the foetid meat and succumbed. Hesitantly I unfastened the lock and entered, carrying the cloth I had soaked in the powerful soporific, which did at least have the beneficial effect of overwhelming the foulness of the air. The outer chamber was empty and I moved stealthily towards the next. I entered the doorway and was met there by a sight that froze the very blood in my veins. The beast was squatting on the floor in the corner, its back turned towards me as it rocked slowly to and fro. Scattered on the floor were decomposed but recognisable remnants of human anatomy, crudely torn and broken. The monster turned its head as it became aware of my presence, and I stared in wild despair and revulsion at the thing that lay cradled in its arms. There was draped the most bloodcurdling travesty of the human form that can be imagined, its rotting limbs strung together with twine that was cutting through the spongy flesh. The head was that of a young girl, blackened with decay and lolling against the creature's naked chest. The bile burned my throat as I fled from the room, pausing only to secure the outer door before rushing outside to gulp in the clean unpolluted air. My head reeled as I sank to the ground, trying to shut the dreadful scene from my mind. The world turned about me like some gigantic carousel and my ears were filled with the roaring and pounding of my own blood, until I felt the darkness press down on me and I slipped to the ground.

August 30th

I awoke damp and shivering in the gathering twilight and wandered all night in the woods around the castle, unable to close my eyes without being overwhelmed by the terrible image that was burned into my brain. Desperately I sought for some explanation of this hideous calamity, but could find none. Somehow the beast has escaped from its confinement, slain the unhappy villagers and dragged them back to its den to mutilate them in this demonic fashion. But why, why? It was like some nightmarish parody of my own work, and with that sudden thought I began to comtemplate an explanation which served also to provide a reason for the increasing restlessness of the monster during the previous weeks. Deep in its grotesque frame must have winked the small and fitful spark of the procreative urge, flickering there unbidden but drawing on the vapours of whatever life-force I had succeeded in simulating. As the vitality of the creature flourished and the flesh healed, its strength also blossomed until the poor, ignorant beast was driven to seek to reproduce itself by the only means it had knowledge of; those it had witnessed executed on itself!

The Vortex

September 3rd

O God, merciful Father, succour me in this dark hour. The scales have fallen from my eyes and I peer into the sulphurous caverns of Hades; loathesome demons pluck and tear at my mortal flesh, and each morning I awake with my nightclothes torn and my skin raw and bruised from the savage beatings I am subjected to. Wherever I may wander in this desolate place, I am hounded by the pack of Hell which seeks to break me and drag me to the throne of its black master. The knowledge that I have been deluded throughout my pitiful life and made the instrument of evil is unendurable. Lord in Heaven, how could you let this cruel thing be done!

I have found the crevice through which the sinister creature slipped on its appalling errands, and have shored it up most securely. Though I cannot bear to approach it directly, some strange compulsion leads me to the door of its chamber where I listen in abject terror to its movements within. Once more that monstrous fluting issues forth from it, tearing at my very soul, and making my breast a battleground whereon the armies of compassion and revulsion are locked in brutal combat. I feel the seed of madness nestling in the dim recesses of my brain.

Where once I saw questing, naked innocence, I now see an evil mind wise in all the ages and ancient in guile. Where once stood the glory of the second Adam, there now stands the awful form of Death made manifest, robed in the unhallowed flesh of men who have already succumbed to his scythe. And yet, in moments of deepest grief, I see the child of my own hands, wrought by the miracles of natural laws from the fabric of which all men are made. Its plaintive cry pleads in innocent perplexity as it casts about its cell, more alone in all the world than I in my most miserable moments have ever been. I long to throw open the imprisoning door and lead it to the light, but each time I stretch forward my trembling hand to throw back the bolts, doubt whispers in my ear to warn me against its cunning appeal. I am lost and afraid.

September 5th

Over the last two days the monster's cries have increased in intensity and altered in tone. At first I believed it to be shedding the cloak of simulated innocence, and hardened my heart against considering its release, but I now have realised that this may not be so. Suppose it is no more than the pitiful, naive creature I had earlier imagined it to be, then its desperate cries could be due to nothing more than its physical hunger, for I have provided no nourishment since I first stumbled on the grisly discovery that still lies within those noisome rooms. Suppose that my fevered imaginings are without foundation! I would be destroying Man's greatest inheritance and the work of my entire lifetime for the sake of a brief delusion, a pathetic fantasy. With the simplest of acts I can either bequeath to Man the priceless gift of eternal life, or open the portals of Hell itself to loose the Horsemen of the Apocalypse upon a fragile world. God alone must decide.

September 6th

I passed the entire night in prayer and contemplation, but no answer came to reveal my course. I cannot make such a decision unaided and must find some compromise until the Lord sees fit to instruct me. I have prepared a large quantity of provender and waited until long after nightfall and the monster's movements ceased. When I was certain that it slumbered, I eased back the bolts and, with my heart pounding so fiercely that I thought it would waken the creature, I opened the door enough to admit the food, then closed and secured it once more. It will be two days before I have to repeat this action, and I pray that my dilemma may be resolved before then. Am I to be Prometheus with the gift of light and death-defeating fire, or Hephaestus who fashioned the deadly Pandora from base clay?

September 9th

Silence fills the castle like smoke, drifting in thick eddies among the corridors and empty chambers. Some fatal moment draws nigh, I am sure of it, and time holds its breath in anticipation. The hellish legions are held in check and have not molested me these last two days. I move about in nervous apprehension, every sound I make seeming to reverberate in the unnatural calm.

Tonight I must prepare a further supply of food for the beast and, with nothing else to occupy me until then, I have spent the hours staring from one of the upper windows. How peaceful is the waiting world. Shadows, like clouds, move softly across the tangled landscape. The thick quilt of forest slopes down towards the town and the shallow pool of humanity that nestles there in blessed ignorance of the dicing for its souls that takes place in this grim pile. The sun slides slowly round the globe as I watch, and by its dying rays I set about the task of readying the creature's provisions.

overleaf
Frankenstein's own sketches of his last creation. In appearance it falls far short of the new Adam he so desperately yearned to make. The limbs are powerful, but the rest of the musculature is disproportionately slack. The stomach, weakened by incisions, is distended; the face fleshless, the eyes blank, the hair sparse and patchy. One leg is wasted.

September 10th

I was forced to sit outside the creature's door for many long hours last night, waiting for it to slip into whatever dreams cavort in its fearsome mind. A pungent odour seeps from within for I doubt that it has the wit to care for itself and there are no civilised facilities therein to accommodate its natural functions. With my courage wound to its tautest pitch, I once more opened the door to set the dishes upon the floor. Against my better judgement, I paused after I had laid down the food, and peered into the gloom. A dark bulk lay huddled in a far corner, its breath rattling sonorously as it slumbered, and as I watched, a tide of compassion rose within my breast for that poor, gigantic child. Lying alone in that squalid neglect lay the fruits of my entire life, the child of science abandoned and imprisoned for gross crimes committed in simple ignorance. My passion stirred my limbs to step towards it, heart and hand outstretched in pity and remorse. The sound of my footstep echoed dully in the heavy air, but before I could take a second pace, there was a flurry of movement of unearthly speed, and to my blinding horror the creature had risen and, even across the room, seemed to tower over me like a black, night-shrouded oak, its eyes gleaming fiercely in the light from the doorway. In an instant it was leaping towards me and, spurred by my own shriek of fear, I leapt to the entrance, slammed the heavy door and threw home the bolts just as the creature's momentum brought it crashing against the wood. A blood-chilling howl rang through the empty halls and out into the night, while tears of terror and agony coursed down my cheeks. I stared, utterly unnerved, as desperate and weighty blows rained furiously against the wood, and the creature bellowed time and time again.

O God, what have I done? Are its mournful wails those of a frustrated avenger, or of a lonely and frightened infant unable to understand the reason for its cruel and total isolation? I stood there for nearly an hour as its roars grew more infrequent and muted, until there was a silence but for the slow, soft shuffling as it withdrew to its bed and lay down once more. Then all was still, and I climbed to by bed-chamber and took a deep draught of Laudanum to quench the bitter fires within me. I know now that if God does not intervene, this murderous dilemma will make me mad.

September 11th

It is not yet light, but I can lay abed not longer. Elizabeth, my sweet Elizabeth has found the door that leads from death to light, and entered my room from that mysterious portal. She could not speak to me, but sat beside my pillow and caressed my fevered brow with hands as cool as the early breeze. I wanted to call out to her, to tell her of the miseries I am cursed with, but my joy had robbed me of speech also. Smiling, she rose and stepped lightly to the end of my bed, turned and gazed fondly upon me. I tried to ask her forgiveness for having cast her from my mind since that dreadful night an eternity ago, but I had not even the strength to raise my head. She tilted her fine head as if in understanding, and raising her hands to the neck of her gown, began to part it in tender passion. But, dear God, it was not the silken gown that parted, but her very flesh, and as the bone and glistening entrails appeared her eyes seemed to flame from within, growing as bright as the fires of hell and draining the life from my body. As I watched, a scream lodging still-born in my throat, her face shifted and melted to form the image of the creature that I had incarcerated below. It grew massive in the darkness, saliva flecking its bloodless lips as it moved soundlessly towards me. I could not stir, and the vast shape loomed over me, then descended to lie upon me, its ghastly face against mine. I felt my ribs cracking beneath its weight until I could no longer draw breath, and as my lungs collapsed, merciful darkness closed over me and I knew no more. When I opened my eyes next, most of the day had already passed and the bloody sun was low over the edge of the world. I rose, weak and chilled, uncertain whether I had dreamed or not, so vivid were the visions that so brutally assailed me. Though I am weary unto death, I cannot bring myself to enter that dismal chamber and sit beside the fireplace, surrounded by every lamp that I can find to keep the shadows at bay.

September 13th

I have not fed the creature. And I know that I shall not do so again. I have fought this battle alone for too long, and shall let God decide the outcome. The agony of compassion that tormented me has ebbed away, and I recognise that it was but a cunning ruse to bring about its release from the chambers below. Locked within those walls is the very spawn of Satan. I am blind no longer, and see with blinding clarity that I was chosen as the instrument of Man's destruction, not his salvation. Little wonder that my most earnest prayers were unanswered!

September 17th

I believe that I shall now be forced to endure the hardest trial of all those that have been forced upon me. The time for subterfuge is past, and the blood-red banners of Beelzebub are unfurled as he renews his onslaught on my mind. He must destroy me to preserve the fiendish changeling that I cradled, but I shall endure till I am certain that the monster has drawn the last particle of nourishment from its evil carcass and has expired. The nocturnal sallies against the frail citadel of my mind have recommenced with frightful vigour, and harass me at intervals throughout the day. I have to take the greatest care over the simplest daily tasks, as they now seek to turn my own body against me. As I walked upon the parapet, a deadly attraction drew me, against my will, to the edge. As I gazed down that dizzying precipice, the wish to step boldly from the crumbling stonework caught me unawares and I was forced to fall upon the ground to avoid dashing myself on the rock beneath.

Hideous fiends lurk in every shadowed crevice of this place, and I am forced to restrict my movements to avoid confrontation. Even from the upper chambers, I can hear the growing frenzy of the starving beast as it seeks to escape the sentence I have passed upon it. It pounds upon the door and tears at the barred windows as hunger gnaws at its belly. God grant that its end is swift, as I find its suffering distressing in the extreme. However this cosmic struggle is resolved I fear that neither of us will survive.

September 18th

The beast has been without food for a week now, but there is no apparent diminution in its strength, and it continues in its furious attempts to escape the slow and remorseless fate the I have imposed upon it. I am fearful lest the wooden door, stout though it is, eventually succumbs to the monster's powerful onslaughts, and I have placed my stoutest furniture against it as an additional precaution. With good fortune, the con-stitution of the creature will weaken faster than that of the barricade. I have abandoned hope of sleep at night and pace through the castle in an attempt to hold the dire visions at bay. Such respite as I must have is snatched during the daylight hours, when the Dark Powers are at their weakest. The surfaces of the rooms seem to shift in a most disturbing fashion as I walk from one to another each night, and they frequently cause me to stumble.

September 26th

Another week has passed, and at last the vitality of the beast appears to be somewhat reduced. Its assaults against the imprisoning doors are much less frequent, and though still intense they are of briefer duration. I am also more confident of survival in my own bitter war, and have discovered an effective counter to the malignant

forces that strike at me from the darkened corridors. As I catch sight of them waiting to spring at me from the black crevices and doorways, I have taken to stealing the initiative and, uttering a bellow of simulated rage, I hurl myself directly at them, whereupon they vanish immediately. Clearly they are unprepared for such an action, and I take delight in discomfiting these hideous beings by turning their own weapons against them.

The creature's den was situated below the laboratory. Frankenstein confined the monster to these quarters when his authority over it began to diminish.

September 29th

Victory has been snatched from me at the eleventh hour. As I prepared to steal some rest from my nocturnal vigil at the break of day, a rending crash rang out from the level below and my breath caught in my throat at its awful significance. The beast was free! Terror gripped my heart in its chill grasp and threatened to crush the life from my breast, as a triumphant wail echoed up the passageways, followed by the sounds of splintering wood as it tore apart the door to its gaol. I sank to my knees, unable to bear my own weight in the face of this final calamity.

I expected to hear at any moment the beast's soft and heavy tread as it came to wreak its revenge upon the one who not only gave it the crude semblance of life but also so nearly succeeded in bringing it to death's dark chamber. But moments passed, and nothing approached me. I raised my head and was straining to catch a sound of the beast when there came a noise from the direction of the storeroom. I sprang to my feet with the realisation that the creature's first thought after its escape would be to satisfy the unendurable hunger that gnawed at its belly. It would have no other thought, and with this truth ringing in my mind, I ran as fast as my uncertain limbs would allow towards the store. Drawing near, I slowed, and proceeded with the utmost stealth until I was close by the heavy door which led from there to the rest of the building. I trembled in horrid anticipation as I peered round the stout frame. There I perceived it crouched on the stone-flagged floor, tearing at one of the large hams that had been hanging there. I had to reach right into the room in order to grip the edge of the door, but the beast was too occupied to be aware of my movement. As my trembling fingers took a purchase on the wood, however, it suddenly discerned my presence and, hurling the meat aside, sprang to its feet with a furious cry that almost froze me to the spot. I threw myself backwards and the door slammed shut a mere second before the huge weight of the monster crashed against it. Though it bowed visibly beneath the impact, it held firm, and I breathed once more as I fought to regain control of my pounding heart.

The beast's appetite was obviously far from satisfied, for after a few desultory blows it ceased, and I heard it shuffling back into the room. I pressed my ear to the door and could hear it resume its feast. The respite allowed me to review the geography of the castle, until I was certain that although the creature had gained access to a substantial supply of foodstuffs, it was no more at liberty that it had previously been, for there was no egress elsewhere in the portion it now occupied. The food that lay within would last for some days, but no more. I must devise some additional defence before the monster renews its attempts to gain its freedom. I can waste no time and shall set to at once to invent some effective measure.

September 30th

I worked throughout the rest of the day and for most of last night to prepare the scheme I have decided upon. I

d. 27 April

Bemerkte heute, wie ich an der Tür vorbeiging, die zu den Zimmern des Tieres geführt, einen unangenehmen Geruch. Ich habe Angst, es frißt nicht all das Fleisch, das ich ihm durch die Wände liefere. Und wenn es einige der verrotteten Fleischreste von ~~Fußbaden~~ frißt und dann erkrankt. Weiss nicht, wie ich Zugang bekommen kann. Ich muss in der Tür ein Loch schneiden und das Tier dazu verlocken, einen Schlaftrunk zu nehmen. Schwierig, da im Zimmer schon Wasser zum trinken ~~zur~~ Verfügung steht.

d. 28 April

Meine Arbeit an der Tür wurde durch noch einen Besuch von dem richterlichen Beamten unterbrochen. Es ist noch eine Person vom Dorf auf rätselhafte Weise verschwunden. Man scheint immer fester entschlossen, ich sei dafür verantwortlich. Man verlangte Eintritt, um sich zu vergewissern, dass der Bösewicht nicht da sei. Das konnte ich nicht zulassen. Wurde schließlich gezwungen, ihnen die Tür vor der Nase zuzuschlagen, um wieder an die Arbeit unten zu gehen.

Die Arbeit endlich fertig, blickte ich in die ~~Dunkel~~heit jenseits der Tür hinein, konnte aber nichts mehr als einen Teil des Zimmers zu sehen bekommen. Drinnen ist ~~die~~ oft schwer

sorely missed the assistance of Igor as I laboured to move some of the electrical equipment from the laboratory to the door in question. At length I succeeded, however, and it was an easy matter to connect it to the ironwork which binds the stout timbers of the door together. It is a petty device, but will serve to make the breaching of it a trifle harder. That it was effective to at least a small degree was evidenced by the howl of consternation that issued forth upon the beast's latest attempt to breach it. I doubt that the creature has sufficient wit to appreciate that it is only the metal portions that are so charged, so it may desist entirely. I feel as though some curious transformation has taken place in my character. Somehow the act of working in the laboratory once more has settled my mind, and I feel as though I have been pulled back from a great abyss which threatened to swallow me. And yet I know the deadly danger that pervades the heavy air of this place is no illusion. For whatever sad reason, the beast and I are now bitter enemies, and there can be no resolution of this matter until one of us falls victim to the other. If I am the loser, there will be something unholy at large in the world. If I am the victor, I will have undone the culmination of my life's work and there will be no reason for me to linger in this meagre and unhappy life.

October 1st

I sat until late into the night upon the castle walls, watching the streaming clouds flutter like banners across the face of the moon. A melancholy procession of memories paraded before my mind's eye as though in farewell, and I contemplated each with gentle sorrow as strange islands encountered in my lonely voyage through the uncharted sea that is life. My tragedy is that of misdirection. I face the unavoidable truth that my life, once a unique and wondrous tree that towered above all others, has in the fullness of its season brought forth a poisonous fruit, and must now be cut down before its seed is disseminated throughout the garden. Though it shames me utterly, I must also recognise that I do not even possess the potency to undo alone these things that I have brought about, but must call upon others to assist me. Tomorrow I shall write to my brother, for if he will aid me the terrible consequence of my arrogant endeavours will be hidden from the mass of men at least, and they will be preserved in innocence of the tragedy that I have wrought.

October 2nd

My letter to Ernest explains only that I have urgent need of his assistance in a matter of the utmost gravity, and entreats him to journey here without delay and in complete secrecy. Though I explained that it would be an adventure of singular danger, I did not dare to provide further explanation, and can only hope that he trusts me not to have exaggerated the significance of the matter. I walked to the town and commissioned a fellow to journey to Geneva to deliver the letter by hand to my brother, for I dare not risk its contents being revealed to any other. I lingered only long enough to purchase a quantity of provisions, as I will otherwise share the fate I have tried to impose on the monster. The local people could almost have knowledge of the grim battle that rages in the solitary fortress that lofts its head above the high forest, for they turn their eyes from mine, yet stare after me as I pass them by. Not one of them would assist me with the heavy parcel of food that I purchased.

When at last I did struggle back through the dripping woods to the summit, I paused on the edge of the forest. My mind recalled the day, so very long ago, when I first set eyes upon this place. How different was my impression of it then, how jubilant my spirits in contemplation of its time-stained walls. With weary tread I wander towards the ancient gate and commit myself to the gloom that yawns beyond. I set a chair and table beside the storeroom door, and light a lamp to illuminate my solitary vigil. My lassitude is so great that I feel no semblance of fear in this unnatural watch. I stare blindly into the darkness beyond the glow of the light, my isolation made still more complete by the total absence of any sound other than that of my own breathing. I try to picture the being that lurks behind that time-weathered wood, but the image shifts and blurs and I can no longer see it. God speed you to me, Ernest, for I think I am dying.

October 4th

The end is drawing near, and I think it will all be over with me before Ernest arrives here. God forgive me, but I have done all I can to bring an end to the iniquity I unwittingly brought about. Others must now conclude what I have been unable to prevent. I am imprisoned in my bedchamber with what food remains from my last excursion into the town, while the monster is loose in the castle and evidently determined to destroy me, for it has made no attempt to venture outside the gate. Its intelligence exceeds my expectations and has increased my burden of guilt. As soon as it had realised that it would not breach its prison by brute force alone, it withdrew; not in the sorry recognition of an inevitable fate, as its silence led me to suppose, but in order to devise a sly and cunning alternative. While I sat in mute self-pity outside the still chamber, the monstrous being was secretly at work elsewhere in those dark apartments. Stealthily and

Frankenstein's creation spent many hours staring out from the battlements of the castle, and this sketch was made during one of his eerie vigils.

with hideous patience it picked at the damp, rotting stone that encompassed its tiny realm. Then today, as I took my seat and prepared myself for another bleak and solitary watch, I heard, but gave no import to an occasional scurry of small sounds from the depths of the corridor behind me. My mournful reverie was finally interrupted by a curious grating noise, as of stone rubbing harshly on stone, but it ceased almost as soon as I had detected it. I listened intently but it did not occur again until I had once more lapsed into my waking dream. Then a noise of a very different quality finally provoked me into turning my head. Shock hit me like a fierce blow, for what I had perceived as no more than a spot of deeper shadow was in fact a breach in the masonry of the wall, from which was uncoiling the huge and terrible mass of the monster itself. As I stared, transfixed with abject fear, it drew itself upright until it almost filled the passage. Its eyes gleamed in the lamplight as though lit from within, and the thin, bloodless lips were stretched across the blackened teeth in the awful semblance of a human grin. I saw in horror the transformation that it had undergone. The yellow and grimy flesh stretched as taut as a drumskin across the facial bones, and the muscles beneath distorted the features grossly. The eyes were sunk so deep in their rimed sockets as to be almost invisible but for the reflected gleam of light. Somehow the nose had been broken since last I had gazed upon this frightful visage, and hair had fallen away in patches, leaving areas of scaly, reddened scalp exposed to view. The stench of decay filled my nostrils as it took a pace towards me, and the movement broke the spell that held me in its grasp. I moaned in horror and threw myself away from the ghastly apparition, upsetting the table and dashing the lamp to the ground as the beast lunged towards me with an eerie wail of hatred. For the first time, fate dealt kindly with me, for the rush of flame from the shattered lamp burst between us and drove the bellowing creature back into the passage. As I hurled myself towards the entrance of the laboratory I could hear the monster lumbering clumsily after me, emitting sharp shrieks of rage which served to spur me on to still greater efforts. At last I was at the door and sprang through, slamming it behind me. I fumbled for the bolts, driving them home at the instant that the monster threw himself against the wood with a resounding crash. I stood back in anticipation of further assaults but none came, and all was silent once more.

October 5th

I do not know what time it may be as my timepiece is damaged, but it hardly matters now. The creature has been at work outside for several hours, and I have no doubt of its intentions. It is fitting that the end should be set among the paraphernalia of the science that brought all this to pass. My concern is no longer that I shall survive this calamity, but that I shall conclude it properly. There are quantities of acid stored here, and I have laboured to construct a primitive device with which to destroy all trace of the horror I have so innocently spawned. There is little point in delaying matters until Ernest's arrival, for there would be nothing he could do to help me now that the beast is abroad, and I cannot add his death to my dismal catalogue of sins. As soon as I have concluded this last entry in my unhappy log, I shall open the door and admit the creature. God's will be done.

Epilogue

What happened after Viktor Frankenstein's last diary entry would be simply a matter for speculation had it not been for an account, apparently rendered by his brother and found with the papers and diaries retrieved by him from the old castle. Whatever his reason for writing it, it does provide a vivid and disturbing corollary to Viktor's own records and illuminates the final episode of a most extraordinary history. Little has been omitted and certainly nothing added to the text reproduced below.

'My brother's letter was welcome proof that he was still living, for we have had no other confirmation since he left the house after the tragic loss of his wife and William, and indeed I had come to think of him as lost. The note begged me to join him in both haste and secrecy, but did not offer any explanation apart from indicating that it was a matter of desperate importance. Viktor is a brilliant man, but given to strange attitudes and fancies, and I felt it wise not to act too precipitously. But though I do not know or understand him well, I appreciated that he could not have appealed to me in this manner without some powerful reason. After long deliberation, therefore, I conceded that whether his distress was real or imagined I would have to answer his appeal, and made ready for the journey. I delayed one day in order to deal with various personal matters, then set off in the company of the fellow who had carried his message. It is a poor time of year for travelling and the journey was tedious in the extreme, but eventually we arrived at a point where my guide indicated the road to the castle, himself refusing to accompany me further. It was a chill, blustery morning made uncomfortable by flurries of light snow. I found myself riding through an unattractive and extensive forest. The path steepened until I was forced to dismount and lead the animal for the last part of the climb. The trees began to thin out and I eventually beheld the castle itself. It is a dismal looking place, and I can now see why my forebear forsook it!

There was no immediate sign of occupation, so I pushed through the tangled undergrowth that bounds the walls and entered via a dilapidated gateway. The courtyard within was no less unkempt, and I was perplexed as to why Viktor should have chosen such a place as his residence. There were no staff to attend on me, so I found suitable quarters for my horse and as the door was unbarred, entered the house. No one answered my call, and I could detect no movement, so after a cursory examination of the adjacent rooms, I ascended the stairs to the next floor. There was a singularly depressing air to the place, an appearance of neglect and squalor which was not in accord with my brother's usually fastidious nature, and I began to sense that, as he had intimated, all was not well. As I looked about, a curious, acrid odour stung my nose, growing more pungent as I advanced down one of the numerous passages. There was clearly little to be gained by continuing to call out for Viktor, so I proceeded in silence, and with some apprehension. I was thankful of a lamp I found in one of the sparsely furnished chambers, as there was little natural illumination. In one portion of the corridor I came upon a curious scene, for several stones had been removed from the wall, and close by a table and chair were overturned and scorched, probably by flames from the lamp that lay shattered on the floor. When I passed my own lamp through the breach in the wall and peered inside, I could see that it had been a kitchen or pantry, and the smell of rotting food was very pronounced. This convinced me that something was very seriously amiss, that either my brother had been forced to flee the house or that he lay helpless in some part of the castle. I strode down the passage, my earlier hesitancy abandoned. As I proceeded, the peculiar stench became oppressive, and I was forced to hold a handkerchief over my nose. It was not a natural scent, and the thought that it was probably one of Viktor's wretched chemicals heartened me, as it was quite possible that he was at work somewhere and was so absorbed that he had not heard my cries. My optimism evaporated, however, when I recalled the abandoned pantry, and, though I am reluctant to admit to it, I began to feel distinctly nervous as to what lay at the end of that gloomy passage. I wished that I had thought to take the pistol from my baggage before entering.

Pressing on, I arrived at a heavy wooden door that lay sightly ajar. Light spilled from the gap into the gloom of the passage and the odour grew more pungent, as I pushed the door wide enough to enter. It resisted my weight; there was evidently some heavy object obstructing its movement from the other side. Putting my shoulder to it, I heaved it aside and stepped into the chamber over the wreckage of some large mechanical device. Light flooded the room from the windows set into the upper portion of the high walls, and I almost dropped the lamp in astonishment at the scene which met my eyes. Machines whose purpose I could not even guess at were scattered about the room, and a system of pulleys led up to an aperture in the ceiling far above. Glass containers such as those used by chemists were much in evidence, together with numerous metal utensils. But the object which gripped by attention and dominated the entire chamber was a web-like tent of silvery filaments which soared to the highest part of the room and

This photograph of Hilde Friedrich, the mother of the child abducted by Viktor Frankenstein, was taken towards the end of her life.

disappeared into a mass of larger ducts, leading in turn to some of the strange mechanical apparatus around the wall. The lower portion was obscured by an enclosure fashioned from silken material, which formed a complete square pierced by the gleaming threads. A most eerie humming pervaded the room as though a thousand insects were on the wing nearby, and through the acrid odour I could discern a more pleasing scent not unlike that experienced in the vicinity of a large waterfall. I could only stand and gaze about me in amazement, all thoughts of seeking my brother's whereabouts momentarily forgotten.

As I stared about me, my eyes fell on something hidden by the wreckage that had obstructed my entrance, and I stepped forward to see what it was. The instant I beheld the object that lay there on the floor, I felt as though my stomach had been turned inside out. I am a soldier and have seen things that would distress a more sensitive creature, but never anything as ghastly as the remains that lay before me. My first thought was that I had at last discovered the fate of my unfortunate brother, but the dimensions of the body, or rather of what remained of the body, were not those of any human being that I had ever seen. The bones, lying in a putrescent soup of liquefied tissue, were unnaturally large and heavily formed. The lower portion was largely undamaged, though areas were blistered in an unusual fashion, as though spattered by molten metal. The upper part was dreadfully mutilated, almost the entire skin surface having been dissolved or eaten away, and the bones protruded grotesquely from the mass of putrid muscle and destroyed organs. The contorted position suggested that the poor creature had suffered the most agonising death imaginable, and there were signs that its demise had been far from swift. The smashed equipment and litter of glass were evidence that it had remained conscious long enough to wreak considerable havoc before succumbing to the fearsome injuries that it had sustained.

How or why such a dreadful occurrence had taken place defied examination, but the question uppermost in my mind was the fate of Viktor, for there was little doubt that he had been involved in this dreadful scene. With great trepidation I began to look about me for some clue, expecting at any moment to stumble over his similarly grisly remains, but no such monstrosity lay upon the stone floor. I then approached the bizarre tent-like structure, and with a determined heave pulled back the flap set in one side. For the second time in this nightmarish adventure, I recoiled with shock. Enmeshed in that gossamer shroud lay the torn and horribly disfigured body of my brother. Tears of confusion and anger filled my eyes as I stared at the scarcely recognisable, ruined face. What on earth could have taken place in this God-forsaken castle? Suddenly, with an involuntary gasp of horror, I saw the crushed remains of his breast rising and falling with the unmistakable movements of respiration. Blood-tinged mucus bubbled softly in his nostrils, and I watched, transfixed, as blood vessels among the entrails spilling from the ruptured abdomen pulsed with the motion of a beating heart. I could not believe what I knew to be utterly impossible: that a body so broken could sustain any semblance of life. Yet the fact was before me. A violent wave of nausea heaved inside me, and I staggered from the room, a silent scream echoing in my skull. I do not recall my actions during the next few hours, but I eventually found myself standing outside on the battlements, buffeted by the freezing gusts of snow-laden wind. I gripped the parapet until my fingers ached, trying to understand the terrible things that I had seen, but they were beyond my comprehension and I shook my head as if to shed the whirl of images before turning into the house. As I wandered back towards that ghastly chamber, lost in deliberation as to what I should do, I passed the open doorway of a room which was fully furnished. Peering inside I recognised some of its contents, and realised that it must have been my brother's bedchamber. I entered and lit the lamp that stood inside the door, to supplement the weak light cast by the single window. I wandered round the room in a trance-like state, touching the various articles of furniture as I passed, as if physical contact with Viktor's possessions would somehow enlighten me as to the cause of his living death.

It was then that I discovered the great pile of papers and notebooks on the table beside the bed. They comprised a diary of sorts, the most recent entries uppermost, and I began to read them with increasing concentration until I could hardly move my eyes speedily enough. Hours had passed before at last I raised my head, and the sky was already beginning to darken. If what I had read was a true record of events, and I had the greatest difficulty in believing that it was, then the terrible story was yet unfinished. The derelict and broken carcass that lay beneath that gossamer canopy had somehow dragged itself on to the waiting couch, painfully and deliberately introduced the delicate filaments into its tissue, and set the complex of machinery in motion. Whatever evil force my brother had discovered and used to create a hellish being, he was at this very moment feeding on to keep his remains throbbing in a hideous mockery of life. I am no scientist, and do not pretend to understand even the smallest significance of the events that have come to pass in this desolate place, but as a human being and a kinsman, I knew what must be done. Though my heart quailed at the prospect of returning to that terrible room, I forced myself to enter it once more and walked with faltering step to where Viktor's broken and lacerated body lay. Terrified and uncertain as to what might occur, one by one I plucked the fine threads of metal from the torn flesh. I had removed no more than half of them when to my utter dismay the yellowed eyes turned towards me, the shattered jaw moved and a hideous murmuring came from the bloodied wreckage of the mouth. I wanted desperately to run from the room, but somehow a new determination seized me and, unable to turn my gaze from his, I continued to pull the filaments from the quivering flesh. The entire body began trembling and the gargling sound increased in intensity, until the back arched into a taut bow then slumped back and was still. Whatever force had been contained in that body had departed, and I turned slowly away.

After a brief search, I returned to the room with as much oil as I could find and poured it over everything there. It was dark as I rode down through the woods, but the shadows danced and leapt like demons as bright tongues of flame licked from the windows of Schwarzstein and crackled in the snow-laden air.'

Located in a solitary corner of the churchyard of Schwarzstein, this unmarked tomb marks the last resting place of Igor, whose remains were removed from the castle courtyard after the fire. A local superstition states that separated lovers will be able to commune if one of them passes an entire night beside the stone slab.